CHRISTMAS IN NEW YORK

NYC HOLIDAY STORY COLLECTION

MELISSA HILL

NOTE

This book was written, produced and edited
in the UK, where some spelling, grammar
and word usage will vary from US English.

CHRISTMAS IN
NEW YORK

"I still can't believe I'm spending Christmas in New York," Penny laughed, rubbing her hands together to warm them.

A tall slender blonde in fitted light blue jeans and a red puffa jacket, she walked towards the kerb where an awaiting black town car stood with an open door. Her boots left prints in the fresh snowfall.

"Why not? And what better way to spend it - and your birthday too," her best friend Kate replied as they neared the car, elation reflected in her honey-coloured eyes. Her diminutive frame was curvier than Penny's, the reward of motherhood.

Their breaths came in wisps as they spoke, filling the area around them with a quickly-evaporating fog

"Besides, what were you going to do in London all alone?" she added.

"I wouldn't have been alone," Penny defended, but they both knew better.

Penny was a workaholic. She had been ever since her fiancé's death three years before.

It had been difficult for her ever since, being part of a world without Tim. Kate knew that.

Over the years she'd tried her best to pull her friend out of the recesses and back into the sunlight where she belonged, but Penny was stubborn. She always had been.

It had taken desperate measures on Kate's part to get her on the flight over from London.

"So where's Ian?" Penny asked, referring to Kate's husband.

"He's meeting us at home. He has some things to get done before he heads back." Kate's words were punctuated by the slamming of the trunk of the town car.

Penny's single suitcase was securely tucked inside, right next to her son Toby's stroller.

"So what happened to your SUV? I thought you loved that thing," Penny asked as she approached the open passenger door. The vehicle's driver was standing sentinel as her eyes grew large at the sight of the interior of the expensive Lincoln.

"I do, but where we are now makes it difficult for me to find parking. The car comes with Ian's job, we just never had a reason to use it before," Kate answered as both women slid into the backseat one after the other.

The door closed behind them.

The warm scent of vanilla greeted Penny as she slid around making herself comfortable. She wasn't used to being chauffeur driven and she fidgeted in the small space.

There was an ice bucket and two champagne flutes tucked into a holder. The glasses alone must have cost more than her coat. She would have much rather preferred Kate's Range Rover. At least she wouldn't be afraid to break something.

"It's great that you both were able to get the holidays off together. I know last year was a bit of a mess."

"Yeah well, you know how corporate types can be – all work, work, work."

"No I don't," Penny mused lightly. "I always liked the blue-collar guys – the kind who work with their hands."

She looked out the window as they pulled away from the airport. As a masseuse, Tim had been great with his hands, and very attentive. He always knew when she was tense and was quick to alleviate the problem.

He was a master at working out the knots from her neck and back, not to mention his stellar foot massages. She missed them. She missed feeling pampered and cared for.

Tim had been her entire world. Having been an orphan, Penny wasn't used to having people care for her, but Tim had, he'd loved her through a time when she could barely love herself.

Then he was gone, and everything she'd hoped for died with him.

"I have to pick up Toby from my mother before we head home," Kate interjected, knowing her friend's thoughts had strayed.

Penny wasn't difficult to read, especially for

someone who knew her as well as Kate. The pair had been best friends since kindergarten, both born and raised in a quiet suburb of London until Kate had gone to New York to attend university.

It was where she'd met Ian Jarvis, her husband. She was studying interior design and he, finance. The artist and the businessman, an unlikely pair, but the two made it look effortless the way they seemed to read each other's minds.

Now they had a house in Middlesex County, a beautiful two-year-old son and careers they were both proud of.

They were the image of the ideal couple.

"I can't wait to see my godson." Penny offered Kate a bright smile to mask her short trip down memory lane. "I bet he's gotten so big since I last saw him - on Skype wasn't it?"

"Yes, nasty thing. A weak excuse for human contact." Kate wrinkled her nose and Penny felt the tirade even before her friend started. "You know how I feel about those things. All the social media that make us 'closer' to the point that we forget to actually speak to one another. Ten people in a room and they're all glued to their smartphones! No one even bothers to look up. It's ridiculous!"

"I know you hate them Kate, but they do serve a good purpose –"

"I miss the days of conversation. I loved it when people got together for dinner and talked about important things – life, future plans. Now it's all posting pictures of the food to Facebook and taking selfies for your Instagram. I swear if it wasn't for my manager demanding I have a social media presence, I promise you'd I'd never twit."

Penny chuckled as she leaned back. "It's tweet, Kate. Tweet. You tweet on Twitter."

"Whatever, you know what I mean."

Kate, the anti-social media activist was a woman who still wrote in her diary instead of a blog.

She posted letters rather than emails if she had a choice, and painted when the entire world had gone digital. Her best friend was a woman from another time and Penny loved her.

CHAPTER 2

"I thought we were going to your house?" Penny commented when it became clear that they weren't headed for the usual turnpike.

Toby was snuggled in his car seat between them, fast asleep. His head rose and fell peacefully against his chest.

"Oh no, we're staying in Manhattan at the moment. Didn't I mention that? The house is being renovated and Ian didn't want Toby in all that dust," Kate replied as she sipped from her bottle of Evian.

She wordlessly offered Penny a bottle, which was politely refused. She'd had enough warm liquids on the plane and couldn't hold another.

Penny responded with disappointment. She was looking forward to getting out of the city setting and enjoying some fresh air. London was a concrete jungle she'd been in her entire life.

"Where are we staying then?"

"At the Easton - on the Upper West Side. Ian's company owns a few apartments there and they offered us one."

"Nice. The perks of being a top performer I take it."

"What can I say, he works hard. He's always at the office. I swear if I didn't know I could trust my husband, I'd believe he was cheating, but affairs aren't something I have to worry about."

The confidence in Kate's voice was awe-inspiring. Penny wasn't sure she'd be as confident if the shoe was on the other foot.

Tim hadn't had late nights, but he did have a lot of female clients. She would have been lying if she said that she'd never had a niggling of fear and insecurity when it came to his fidelity – but she was told that insecurity was common for children who'd been raised in the social services.

Insecurity, doubt and fear – the three deadly plagues. Penny had suffered from all of them at some point in her life, insecurity being the worst of the bunch.

When she met Tim she was convinced she didn't deserve to be happy. That people like her didn't get the happy ending.

She'd pushed him away but he wouldn't give up. He pursued her until she relented, earning her trust every step of the way.

He proved to be the best of men – the best man she'd ever known. It was unfair that such a wonderful life should be snuffed out by the callousness of a one-armed man, who wanted the contents of a supermarket's register.

Tim had been in the wrong place at the wrong time, getting a bottle of wine to celebrate their fourth anniversary. In the blink of an eye, his life came to an end and Penny's beliefs about happy endings were proven true.

"It must be nice having the life you always wanted. Remember growing up you always said you'd move to New York one day and become a famous designer?" She offered a warm smile of admiration. "You really did it, Kate."

"I'm not famous," her friend countered as they pulled up outside the salubrious apartment building. "But I am happy," she continued, smiling at her sleeping son.

When her eyes returned to Penny they glistened slightly as her voice quivered. "I want you to be as happy, Pen."

"I am –"

"No you're not –"

Their conversation was interrupted as the passenger door was pulled open and their driver stood waiting.

He already had Toby's stroller out and unfolded.

Penny gave Kate a placating look before stepping out of the car. A light snowfall was just beginning and passersby huddled down in their coats and jackets.

She pulled her coat closer around her neck as Kate bundled up Toby.

"We better get inside. I don't want him getting a cold," her friend stated as she held her son to her chest, shielding him from the nipping wind.

The doorman had the door ready upon their approach and Penny followed her friend into the exquisite lobby. The driver followed behind them like a lost puppy, with Penny's luggage in hand.

The Easton was a testament to Upper East Side design and elegance. The building had every amenity imaginable and a view to kill for.

Penny was dumbstruck as she was given the tour of Kate's three-bedroom, two-bath apartment. The kitchen looked like something off of the cover of *Better Homes and Gardens*. Her small one-bedroom with pokey fireplace was the ugly stepchild in comparison.

I bet that's real marble. What the hell am I doing here?

Penny was still asking herself that question as she sat in the living room skimming through magazines as Kate got Toby settled down again. He'd woken fifteen minutes earlier and seemed fractious.

"Sorry about that. He can be a bit cranky when he has an accident," Kate commented as she took a seat beside Penny.

They looked at each other in silence, their

earlier exchange the proverbial elephant in the room.

Finally, Kate broke the discomfort. "Look, you know me. I can't hold my tongue and discretion isn't my strong point so I'm just going to say it."

"Kate –"

"You aren't happy Pen," Kate's eyes began to smart with tears.

Penny felt the sting of panic well up inside her. She couldn't handle tears, especially not Kate's.

"You haven't been for a long time, and I'm worried about you." She locked her gaze on Penny. "Ever since Tim died you've been a different person. You barely laugh. You don't go out. All you ever do is work. You even stopped calling Tim's parents."

Penny's eyes widened. "How on earth did you know that?"

"Mrs. Walters gave me a call when you stopped returning hers. She's worried about you too Pen. We all are."

"You don't have to worry I'm fine," Penny replied tersely. She hated people talking about her behind her back. "Since when do you and

Colleen talk to one another? I don't remember either of you ever doing that when Tim was alive."

"Don't," Kate cautioned, sensing the shift. "Don't make this into some kind of conspiracy. I gave her my number at Tim's funeral. She kept it. When you stopped calling and returning their calls she was worried, so she contacted me. How else was anyone going to know if you were alright? I barely know half the time."

"That's not fair Kate. You know I can't stand to see you cry," Penny blubbered as they embraced.

"I can't help it. I'm just so worried about you and I love you."

"I love you too, and I'm sorry I made you worry. It was just … easier to keep to myself after Tim's death. It didn't hurt so much when there weren't so many reminders of when I was happy."

Kate held her at arm's length. "Tim wouldn't have wanted this. You know that. You need to let yourself be happy again."

"I know," Penny replied as she wiped her cheek with the back of her hand.

"He wouldn't have wanted you to stop living."

The two women fell into another embrace, the comfort of their friendship easing away the tension of the years of imposed emotional distance.

They were still sniffling when Ian and his guest arrived.

"So the Junko contract is still pending? I thought Morrissey was pushing that for Christmas. I spent the past six months having no social life to get that done because the company 'needed' the deal to go through ASAP. It's spent the past three weeks on that man's desk. Now you're telling me it's on hold until the New Year?" Mike Callaghan's voice filled the empty corridor as he and Kate's husband Ian, disembarked the elevator.

Each at over six feet tall and with similar wide set jaws and unruly spiked medium brown hair, Ian and Mike could have passed for a twin at a distance.

On closer inspection the differences were evident.

Ian's chestnut eyes were set into a slimmer more serious face, though the five o'clock shadow matched Mike's perfectly.

Mike's softer appearance gave him a more boyish look with his blue eyes and dimpled chin.

Ian was wearing his customary tailored grey suit with a navy tie and leather shoes, while Mike was dressed in dark jeans, a light blue buttoned-down and a light grey vest. He wore loafers on his feet and the top button of his shirt was undone.

"I tried to get him to move on it but he's stalling. You should probably drop a hint to Nolan, just to cover yourself," Ian stated as he turned his key in the lock of the apartment.

"Yeah, I will. Morrissey has been after me for ages. I don't want him trying to put the fault for the delay on me." He followed Ian into the apartment, both continuing their conversation as they walked into the living room.

"Honey, we're home!" Mike joked as he rounded the corner, his slight twang faltering the moment his blue eyes settled on his friend's wife and her guest.

What's she doing here?

"HONESTLY MIKE, the amount of time you spend here people might think you're part of the family," Kate laughed as she stepped towards him, placing a friendly peck on his cheek.

She immediately turned to her husband, giving him his customary smooch.

"Yeah, well it happens when you have no life," Mike joked, glancing in Penny's direction.

"You better get one if you ever intend to make me a godmother someday," Kate retorted, taking Ian's briefcase and setting it aside. She looked at their otherwise empty hands. "I thought you two were bringing home dinner?"

"Don't worry. I called and ordered before I left the office. The delivery guy should get here any second." Ian replied as he promptly removed his tie on his way to their bedroom.

"What did you get?" Kate called after him.

"Chinese," Mike and Ian answered in

harmony before Ian disappeared into the other room.

PENNY WATCHED the cosy display at a distance, suddenly uneasy. She hadn't anticipated there being anyone else at Kate's tonight.

She was hoping for a quiet night with her friends, not a mini dinner party. This trip was definitely not turning out how she planned.

And who was the guy? He looked familiar but she couldn't place him.

"Penny, you remember Mike - Ian's best friend?" Kate noted the blank look she received and elaborated. "He was the best man at our wedding. You remember Penny don't you Mike?"

Him!

For Penny, the memory came rushing straight back.

Ian and Kate were married only a few months after Tim's death, and she'd spent the entire ceremony and reception trying to keep it together for Kate's sake.

She'd tried to avoid people but weddings weren't exactly a time to be recluse. People found you whether you wanted to be found or not, especially men.

Weddings were magnets for needy singles trying to score. Mike had been one of them.

He'd pestered Penny until she'd finally blown up, promptly telling him how little she cared for his callous advances. That was the first and last time they'd spoken.

"Yeah, I think I do," she replied noncommittally.

"Yeah, she's the woman who bit my head off for asking her to dance," Mike chuckled as he flopped down on the couch.

"You deserved it," she snapped, the unpleasant feelings resurfacing.

"Excuse me?" he continued, leaning forward, the corners of his eyes squinting. "I was being perfectly civil. You were the one having a tantrum."

"You call that civil? What - were you raised in a barn? I told you to leave me alone and you kept harassing me –"

"Asking someone if they'd like a drink and for a dance isn't harassing behaviour last time I checked. And yes, I was raised in a barn. I grew up on a farm in Minnesota; barns were something we had plenty of."

"Well, that explains a lot." Penny was raging ahead full steam, blood rising to her cheeks as her hands clenched at her sides.

How dare he act all innocent and try to make her look like a petulant child?

"Okay you two, time out," Kate interjected, stepping between them, her hands in a makeshift T.

She looked at the equally annoyed faces, "Both of you please keep your voices down," she scolded, as she stifled her own. "Toby is asleep in the other room and I'd like it to stay that way for a while longer."

As if on cue the toddler's voice erupted in a scream and Kate settled a scathing look upon each of them before marching towards the nursery. "Don't let me hear another word from you two," she warned before going to tend to her son.

Penny and Mike exchanged curt looks.

Insufferable.

ANNOYING.

By the time she rejoined them, Penny had found a spot in an armchair, a magazine occupying her attention, while Mike was flipping through sports channels for something good to watch.

The buzzer rang.

"Great, dinner's here!" Ian stated as he stepped out of the bedroom, smoothing down the front of his polo. "What did I miss?"

Three pairs of annoyed eyes settled on him, but no one answered.

CHAPTER 4

*D*inner had been far from spectacular.

Penny and Mike refused to say more than the basic necessities to one another.

Pass the rice. Where's the wontons?

Everyone felt the tension until Penny finally excused herself, citing fatigue from the flight as the culprit.

It wasn't true of course. She just needed space.

She had come to New York with expectations of a dream weekend away from normal life, but so far it was a nightmare.

She loved Kate and Ian and adored their relationship, but being in their home and seeing their family and how easily Mike seemed to fit into the picture, made her realize just how alone her existence was.

She didn't have anyone to greet her when she got home. Not even a cat. There was no child to cuddle or friend who was part of the family. She was alone. Her entire world was her work, but it didn't keep her warm at night.

WHEN SHE WOKE the next day a delicious aroma welcomed her. She would have wandered out in search of the morsels that were waiting, but the fact that she'd slept in her clothes from the day before was a problem.

She made quick work of a shower, slipping into a pair of red leggings and a cream cashmere sweater before making her way to the kitchen.

"Good morning," she greeted, feeling a bit better after her rest.

"You mean good afternoon," Kate replied as she bounced Toby on her hip. The toddler's face was smeared with some kind of green goo. There were flecks of it in Kate's hair. "It's after one," she added.

"You're kidding? I slept that long? I never sleep that long."

"You never sleep, that's why you needed the rest." Kate wrinkled her nose in Penny's direction. "Lunch is over there," she pointed with her head as she tried to give Toby another spoonful of peas. "I ordered Italian. Thought you'd like it."

Penny chuckled as she poked at the containers of food. "Do you ever think you'll learn to cook?"

"Never. Ian cooks, the maid cleans and I make the place look spectacular. Match made in heaven," she mused.

Penny returned to the comfort of the armchair she'd occupied the night before, folding her leg beneath her. "Where's Ian this morning?" It was Saturday so hardly at work.

"He and Mike went to get the tree. They should be back soon."

Penny huffed. "Is Mike coming over again?" she asked between forkfuls.

"More than likely. He lives one floor down. Why?"

"Nothing," she pouted. A moment later Kate's chuckle got her attention. "What?"

"I was just thinking about you and Mike." She gave Toby another spoon of baby food.

"What about Mike and me?" Penny asked, sitting up.

"Just that you two are so much alike –"

"I am nothing like that guy. He's pigheaded and opinionated. Can you imagine him suggesting that *I* was acting childish at the wedding? He was the one being an opportunist. Trying to hit on me like that after…"

Kate looked over. "After Tim?" she finished, her voice gentle. "Pen, he couldn't have known that."

Penny remained silent, her food momentarily forgotten.

"We didn't tell anyone about Tim. I know you like your privacy, and I didn't want people…I didn't want you to be uncomfortable, so Ian and I agreed to keep that to ourselves. No one knew."

Still, she remained silent.

"I've known Mike a long time and he's isn't that kind of guy. He'd never take advantage of someone vulnerable, especially if he knew. If he wanted to get you a drink or asked for a dance, it's because he wanted to."

She wiped Toby's mouth. He'd had enough for the day. "I'm going to get him cleaned up. I'll be right back."

Penny watched as Kate and Toby went into the other room, leaving her alone with her thoughts.

She'd never considered that Mike's actions may have been anything but unscrupulous. The fact left her unsettled. She was still contemplating it when Ian, and the man himself, arrived with tree in hand – arm.

CHAPTER 5

*H*e couldn't stop thinking about her.

Ever since their verbal tug-o-war Mike couldn't get the thought of Penny from his mind.

The thoughts had escalated to guilt by the time he and Ian returned to the Easton. Ian had explained, though reluctantly, what had instigated Kate's best friend's caustic reaction three years earlier, and why it would have ignited her ire the night before.

Mike knew that pain all too well.

The moment his eyes settled upon her, seated the in same chair as the night before, he wanted to say something, to apologise.

If he had known, if he'd had even an

inclining what Penny had been going through at the wedding three years ago, he would have left her alone.

He knew what it was like to have people hovering around you, wanting things from you when all you wanted was to be alone. Hide.

"Where's Kate?" Ian asked as he and Mike shuffled into the living room with a huge spruce.

"She's cleaning Toby up. Messy lunch." She stood. "Need a hand with that?" she asked, already clearing a path for them, shifting the coffee table out of their way.

She surreptitiously glanced in Mike's direction but said nothing.

"Hey," he murmured as he passed her, helping Ian hoist the tree into place.

"Hi." Her eyes shifted away from him. She returned to her seat.

The next half hour was spent making faces at Toby, while Kate, Ian and Mike tried to get the tree straight in the stand.

"No, it's still leaning," Kate said, tilting her head. "Shift it more in your direction, Mike."

"Penny, can you help us out here? Advise my wife that this isn't a show house, it doesn't have to be straight," Ian called from beneath the bows of the blue spruce.

"Not me." She tickled Toby's nose with her finger. "I know better than to get in Kate's way when she's decorating." Penny continued bouncing the toddler on her knee as Ian struck the table with a red plastic hammer.

"Thank you, Penny. Now...more to you Mike."

BY THE TIME the decorations were brought out, both men were exhausted and Kate was slightly agitated. She liked things to be perfect and hated when it wasn't.

The tree wasn't. It bent to the right.

Ian had picked a faulty tree.

"Don't fret Kate. You can't really tell from the way we have it leaning back like that," Penny tried to pacify her, but it was no use.

She would be put out for the rest of the evening. It was one of those things you either loved or hated about Kate; she was a perfectionist.

As they began hanging the finely crafted ornate balls from each of the willowy bows,

Penny found herself transported to other Christmases.

There was her first real Christmas, with her foster family, O'Connells. They'd been nice to her while she was in their care. They treated her almost like their own until it was time for her to go back.

You never got to settle when you were a foster child. You never really had a home.

It wasn't until she met Kate in her last year of primary school, that Christmas began to have a whole new meaning.

She glanced at her friend as a wave of affection wafted over her. Kate had been her one constant in life, a true friend.

So was her family. They had welcomed her into their home and their lives. Every Christmas, except before they left for New York, she'd spent with them in their Wimbledon home.

As she continued dressing the tree, the last thing Penny expected was to bump heads with Mike. Her forehead collided with his chin.

"Sorry..." they mumbled in harmony, holding each other's gaze for the first time since he'd arrived.

She wanted to say something. She just couldn't. How could she even begin?

Penny didn't want to have to dredge up the past, to explain her behaviour that day – about Tim.

Thankfully she didn't have to.

Mike's eyes twinkled in the sparkling white lights of the tree. He smiled, making the dimples in his cheeks appear. "I …uh… I wanted to apologise for last night. I was a bit of a jerk," he said, kneeling to retrieve the ball she'd let slip from her hand.

Thankfully the soft carpet underfoot had prevented it from shattering.

"No, I was being stupid. I'm the one who should apologise –"

"No, I should." Mike's voice lowered. "I didn't know about …" he faltered for the right words. "I didn't know about your loss."

Penny's eyes grew wide. She glanced over Mike's shoulder to where Kate and Ian were quietly discussing where to hang an ornament.

When her gaze returned to Mike's, she found his hadn't moved.

"Don't be mad. Ian told me earlier. He thought I'd understand."

"How could you understand?" Penny's voice echoed the loneliness of the statement.

"Because I do. And I just want to say I'm sorry. For yesterday, and for three years ago."

He handed her an ornament but said nothing more.

On the other side of the tree, Kate sneezed.

CHAPTER 6

*K*ate was sick.

The cold she'd been so afraid Toby would get from the winter temperatures, had snuck up on her instead, leaving Ian to tend to a very miserable wife and a mewling child who wanted his mother.

It was a little more than the stalwart businessman could handle, having two people vying for his attention.

Penny, seeing his plight, offered to take Toby to the children's playroom downstairs in the building, while Ian tended to the bigger baby upstairs. Kate was never a person who took illness well. While she was the most organised and efficient of people, when sickness struck, she was equally demanding.

"Come on little guy," Penny cooed as she took Toby by the hand and boarded the elevator, pressing the number for the play area.

She watched the numbers on the wall light up as they began to descend. It stopped on the floor below. She stepped aside, pulling Toby towards her, as she waited for the passenger to board. When the doors opened, however, she got a surprise. "Mike."

"Hey there!" he greeted with a smile as he boarded, the large doors closing behind him. He looked down at Toby, "Hey buddy. How're you doing?" he asked, ruffling the little boy's mop of brown curls.

Toby tried to grab his hand in response.

"Where are you two headed?"

He has a nice smile ... Penny found herself thinking as she watched Mike play with her godson.

"Down to the play area," she replied, a strange feeling tickling her insides. She hoped she wasn't coming down with something too. "Kate isn't feeling well this morning so I'm giving Ian some space. What about you? Where're you headed?"

"I was just headed down the street for some coffee, but how about I join you two?" His eyes met Penny's, a smile still tugging at the corners of his lips. "I can keep you company for a while."

Did she want company? She wasn't sure. If she did, did she want Mike's? They had somewhat buried the hatchet in their three-year-long misunderstanding, but that didn't suddenly make them friends. Did it?

He wasn't a bad guy, from what little she'd seen of him, and Kate assured her of his character – and her best friend was an excellent judge. However, it still didn't dispel the strange feeling in her stomach. Something akin to a nervous flutter, but Penny didn't get nervous flutters.

Not in a long time.

"Alright," she finally answered, giving Mike the smallest of smiles. They rode the rest of the way in silence, except for Toby's babblings.

The play area was surprisingly empty when they arrived, but Penny was thankful for it.

"Where is everyone? I was expecting other children to be here. Schools are finished for the holidays," she commented as she let go of Toby's hand and allowed him to wander.

"There probably aren't that many children in this building yet. Besides, the families that do have them usually travel for the Christmas break," Mike replied as he joined Penny at a nearby table, turning his chair to face her.

He couldn't help watching her. Though he tried to be subtle, his eyes kept wandering back to Penny's face.

She was striking. Her oval face, though nondescript, was enhanced by her large almond-shaped eyes and long lashes.

He watched them flutter against her cheeks as she observed Toby playing in the submarine-shaped apparatus. She smiled effortlessly as she watched the child.

It was the first time he'd such a smile from her, so relaxed and unguarded. It was beautiful. He was glad she'd decided to wear her hair back in a ponytail, allowing him to see it.

He hadn't entirely thought this plan through, but the moment he saw her he knew he couldn't let the opportunity slip by him.

Ever since he saw her for the first time, there was something about Penny that captured him. She'd smiled at all the right places, as Kate and Ian exchanged vows, as he watched her from behind Ian's shoulder. She was stunning all dressed in aqua, with her hair swept up in a bun, tendrils framing her face.

He hadn't gotten the chance to say much to her as they processed out of the church, but after, at the reception, he'd tried. He had believed, mistakenly, that her aloofness was because she didn't know anyone at the wedding, having only arrived the night before, missing the rehearsal.

He thought she just needed some prodding to help her relax. He hadn't known then what he knew now.

"How's your day been?" he asked gently.

"Good, if you leave out the sneezing and sniffling coming from Kate's room all morning," she joked.

He liked the sound of her laugh.

"Yeah, Kate can be a bit of a whiner when she's sick," he added. "I was there last year when she got a cold about this time. It was the worst. I don't think I'm even that bad," he chuckled.

"How long have you lived here? In the building I mean?" she glanced back at Toby, who was now trying to kiss the fish mural on the wall.

"Pretty much since it opened. The company took two apartments. I was fortunate to get one. Ian was offered, but having a family he opted to take a house outside of the city. Can't say I blame him; I'd probably do the same." He followed her gaze to Toby, but it was only a moment before it returned to her. "What about you?"

"What about me?" Penny asked perplexed.

"Are you the city type? Or more a suburban girl?"

She considered the question. It wasn't something she'd ever been asked before.

"I guess I'm more of a suburban girl," she smiled wistfully.

"What's that about?" Mike asked, curious to find out what could make her smile.

"Oh, I was just remembering something from when I was young?" She looked at him, and after a while of him continuing to sit silently watching her, she continued, her gaze fixed on the distant memory. "I was raised in foster homes. This one family, the O'Connells, were really great." She played with her cuticles as she spoke. "They had this nice two-storey house in the suburbs of London. It was the first time I'd ever been out of the city proper. It was really nice. No traffic and noise, just peaceful nights and a lawn. I'd never seen a lawn before then."

Mike continued to watch her intently, not wanting to interrupt, lost in her memory.

"Out of all the families I lived with, they were my favourite. They treated me like one of their own, and I guess I came to associate that kind of life with suburbia," she chortled. "Kinda silly isn't it?" She turned to look at Mike then, and her breath caught.

She couldn't describe the look on his face. He seemed engrossed in what she was saying. His eyes were settled on her, but not intrusive as if he was truly listening. Almost like he cared, which was ridiculous.

Mike didn't know her - why would he care? Still, she couldn't help but be transfixed by that look, and for the first time she realised, he wasn't bad to look at.

His eyes were intense, piercing blue. Even with his face still, there was a gentleness in his appearance, despite his overwhelming size, seated in a chair built for children.

"You're staring," Mike commented, his dimples showing.

Slightly startled she replied, "So are you."

"I guess I found something nice to look at." A soft snort escaped him as Penny's face reddened. "Yeah, that was corny," he added.

Penny laughed harder. "Yes, it was." She rose from her seat to collect Toby before he ate one of the fish. Mike followed.

"I was just thinking," he said, standing beside her, waggling his fingers in front of Toby. "You're only here for a few days. You should see the city before the real Christmas rush breaks in. How about I pick you up tomorrow and show you around Manhattan a little?"

Toby stretched out his arms, trying to get from Penny to Mike. She let him go as she considered the invitation. Mike hoisted the toddler above his head, making him giggle, before settling him in his arms.

Penny watched the exchange, which some-how, made her feel more at ease.

"What time?" she asked, laying a gentle hand upon Toby's back.

He smiled. "Lunchtime sound good?"

"I'll be ready."

CHAPTER 7

*C*entral Park was white.

A blanket of snow had fallen overnight, leaving behind a veritable wonderland. The soft powder blanketed everything as far as the eye could see, hanging from tree limbs and obscuring the grass and pathways, leaving only a few naked magnolia trees to contrast the down.

The sun sparkled against the snow, casting the scene in soft light, as families played together and lovers meandered hand-in-hand.

It was magical, and Penny was falling under its spell.

"Not what you were expecting?" Mike

mused beside her, as he chewed his hotdog, which came with all the trimmings.

"No, definitely not what I expected," she answered as they walked, their footfalls in synch. "I would never have pegged you for a hotdog kinda guy."

"Gray's Papaya isn't just a hotdog. It's an experience. One everyone who visits New York should have."

Once again a small laugh erupted from some quiet place inside her, which had long lay dormant. It felt good. Really good.

Penny stuffed the last bit of her hotdog into her mouth, savouring the morsel. Mike had been right, a Gray's hotdog was an experience. She crumpled the remnants into her palm but halted abruptly as Mike's encircled hers. Her breath hitched and her eyes widened, a slight shiver tracking up her arms.

"Let me." Her fingers unfolded without protest, transferring the wrapper from her hand to his.

A small smirk played on Mike's lips as he turned and tossed the wrappers in a nearby bin. She watched him silently before falling into step with him once more.

They walked in companionable silence, neither feeling the need to break it with conversation. Their steps weaved away and towards each other as they moved further into the park.

"It's like walking in a snow globe," Penny whispered to herself as she took in the beauty around her. Winter in New York was very different from winter in London. She couldn't describe how it made her feel – warm, hopeful. She breathed deeply, holding on to the feeling, determining never to let it go, even when she had to go back home.

"Do you like horses?" Mike's voice interrupted. There was a glint in his eye, a playfulness, as he spoke.

"Never really been around them. Why?" Her brow furrowed gently, even more, when Mike grasped her hand and began marching towards a horse and carriage.

He couldn't mean to –

"You will now," he stated.

Penny's stomach flipped, but she didn't resist. Even as he spoke to the driver and offered her a hand to board the all-white buggy, which was lined in red velvet, she didn't protest. Instead, she gripped his hand, looked into his eyes and smiled as she pulled herself up and settled upon the plush bench. Mike was beside her a moment later and they were off.

The moment the horse and carriage moved off Penny felt a thrill run through her. The stately ginger stallion pranced proudly as he pulled, black harness upon his back, his driver bedecked in a black top hat and red tails – quintessentially Christmas, a Santa for Central Park, the carriage his sleigh.

"Who are you?" she mused, her head shaking lightly.

"What'd you mean?" Mike countered, shifting towards her.

"You took me for a hotdog lunch and now a carriage ride through Central Park. You're like some actor from a movie or something." She laughed openly. "I bet you even have the dream life here in New York too." Penny's laughter would have continued if it hadn't been for the look in Mike's eyes, a sadness.

The lump in Mike's throat rose and fell as he swallowed down the memories. He may have wished for the dream life, but he was far from some pretty composition.

He hesitated to speak, searching Penny's face for the answer, but finding it was something closer to his heart that had the reply. He looked away, focusing his eyes on the bobbing of the stallion's head.

"I didn't always live here Penny. I came out here to live with my uncle when I was thirteen," he paused, then continued. "Like I said, I was raised in Minnesota, a little farm near Wright. Growing up there was wonderful." He smiled, a sad smile.

Penny sat back, listening.

"It was me, my dad, my mom and my brother Nathan. Nathan was a great kid. He was two years younger than I was and followed me around like a shadow. Everything I did, he had to do too. I fell, he fell. We were always together. My mother would warn me to watch out for him. And I did. I tried to. But I failed."

"You don't have to –" she whispered, her eyes fixed on the way his jaw tensed. She suddenly wanted to soothe that straining muscle with a stroke of her thumb. She resisted.

"It's okay," Mike interrupted, offering a

weak smile in compensation. "It was a long time ago."

He didn't turn away but avoided her gaze nonetheless.

"We were playing near the creek. Running over the rocks and jumping over logs, typical boy stuff. I was having such a great time, that I didn't notice the larger-than-normal splash from behind me. I just kept running. It was a while before I realised I couldn't hear Nathan anymore." His eyes rose to her face. "By the time I did, it was too late. He'd fallen in and hit his head. My parents sent me to my uncle a couple of months after the funeral. They divorced two years later."

He turned, facing her. "When I said understood, about Tim, I meant it. If I'd known that you were going through that, I would have left you alone. All I wanted after Nathan died was for people to stop asking, and just let me be. It's rough when you lose someone you love. Especially when you were powerless to prevent it – change it. I know that feeling. It took me a long time to get over it, as much as you can."

"I'm sorry Mike." The words left her mouth, even before she thought them. Her hand, like her lips, had acted on their own accord, reaching out to hold Mike's as he spoke. "I had no idea."

"Look, this isn't what I brought you out here for," he offered a smile in recompense. "To share my life's history. I wanted to show you how great life can be when the sadness fades. And it does Penny. It may take a while, but you learn to live again. To let go and go on." He squeezed her fingers gently. "There are moments like this to be had for you, Penny. Carriage rides, great food and pretty decent company," he mused lightly. "But only when you're ready."

She looked at Mike, unable to speak, his words piercing her, and she offered only a smile in return as sounds of the park surrounded them.

The silence that passed between them then, though tinted with some unspoken understanding, recognition of souls who had loved and lost, sparked with something new.

His hand still holding hers.

CHAPTER 8

"*Y*ou like her."

"What?" Mike asked, over a pot of bubbling root vegetables. Ian and Penny were out Christmas shopping, and Toby was at his grandmother's, leaving him and Kate alone.

"Just stating the obvious," Kate replied as she set the table. "You like her. Penny, you do, admit it. I can tell. I can always tell these things." She adjusted the water goblets, ensuring they were perfectly in line.

Mike smiled as he stirred gravy and tasted the rich brown liquid. "Doesn't really matter, does it?"

"Of course it does. If you like Penny, and

she likes you, then there's a chance I can finally get her to move out here. You two can get married and Toby can have a god-brother."

Mike almost choked on the gravy.

"Woah, what are you talking about? Aren't you going a little fast Kate? I mean, Penny doesn't even –"

"Yes, she does. She doesn't know it yet, but she does. She likes you too."

The speed at which Kate crossed the room and stood beside him, must have been some kind of record, her manner conspiratorial. Mike wasn't sure what to make of it.

"Kate?" he eyed her warily, checking the roast meat.

"Mike," she smirked. "Since that little carriage ride of yours, I've heard nothing but questions about you. That's the most she's asked about anyone since Tim." She touched his shoulder, turning him squarely in front of her. Her blue eyes were serious. "So, as her friend I have to say this." Their eyes locked. "If you aren't serious about my friend. If you in any way doubt that you may be interested in her, then walk away now."

"Excuse me?" His brow wrinkled.

"You heard me. Penny is my best friend. She's been inside herself for three years since Tim, and she's finally coming out. I won't let you, or anyone, drive her back in. Understood?" She patted his cheek and grinned. "I love you, Mike, as a brother, but I'd castrate you like Lorena Bobbitt if you hurt Penny. Got it."

He nodded his head, shocked.

"Perfect! Now let's have a very Merry Christmas and get you and Penny together, shall we?" With that, she turned on her heel and returned to her table setting, adjusting the knives.

Mike eyed her uncomfortably.

By the time Ian and Penny returned the table was set, the food was ready and the wine was chilling.

"We're back!" Penny sang as she walked into the living room, boxes and bags in hand. "Something smells great."

"Mike's been cooking up a storm since you left," Kate supplied as she sipped her wine, casually flipping through a magazine.

"You mean dinner isn't takeout?"

"No," Mike's voice drifted past her ear, the

warmth tickling her cheek. "I did everything," he stated as he passed with a basket of hot rolls.

She turned, watching him as he walked over to the table, and despite herself, she smiled.

I have to stop doing that.

She excused herself to put away her purchases, small tokens to take back home and special gifts for Penny, Ian and Toby. When she returned everyone was seated.

The meal was sumptuous, the conversation delightful and the company engaging. They talked and laughed at random, about the beard on the new Macy's Santa Clause to Penny's work with special needs children.

The conversation rolled on at will, the company unguarded. It was the freest she'd felt in a long time, being around people. Mostly Penny stayed to herself. Despite what she had first believed, this trip was turning out a lot better than she'd expected.

By ten o'clock Ian was loading the dishwasher, while Penny and Mike sat beside each other on the carpet, looking through old photo albums.

Kate watched them with satisfaction as she called her mother to check on Toby. Once assured that her son was well and asleep, she put her plan into action.

She yawned exaggeratedly. "Ian, I think we should head to bed now. I'm so tired."

"What? It's only ten –"

"Yes, but I'm sooo tired," she stated, walking over to where he stood and giving him the look. It was one Ian knew well.

"Okay," he stated as he put the last dish in and set the washer. "I guess we're going to bed. Night guys."

He and Kate headed towards the bedroom, while Penny and Mike watched silently as the door closed behind them.

Penny reacted first.

"She isn't very subtle is she?"

Mike chuckled. "Not at all," he replied, his eyes settling on her face. His arm was around her back, resting on the seat of what he'd dubbed her favourite chair, as they poured over photos of her and Kate as children.

"Should I go?" The question was loaded and he knew it. If she wanted him to leave he would, but something in the way she looked at him told him she didn't.

"No," was the gentle response that was

interrupted with a demure smile. "I'd like it if you stayed."

"Then I'll stay."

It may have been only seconds that their eyes were engaged, but in those moments, with those words spoken, Mike sensed that there was more in her invitation than simply a few extra minutes. It was an invitation into her life. An invitation he'd gladly accept.

"Can I get you another glass of wine?"

"Sure."

He grabbed her glass and his and made his way to the kitchen to pour them another round. It was a fine merlot, medium-bodied – a good year.

As he poured he watched Penny. She'd risen from the floor and stood by the tree, admiring the decorations. He couldn't help but think that she looked like she belonged there. She shouldn't be going back to London. She belonged in a place like this, having Christmases like this with friends who loved her. She'd been closed off for so long. He wanted to see her bloom.

"A toast?" He placed a glass in Penny's hand.

"To what?"

"To the end of misunderstandings…and to getting to know each other better."

His eyes sought out the willingness in hers and found it.

"To getting to know each other."

CHAPTER 9

What was this feeling?

Every day since her arrival in New York, he'd been there. Dinner, decorating or just hanging out on the couch, Mike was there.

But today he wasn't. And Penny couldn't describe the feeling.

He wasn't there at breakfast or lunch. He wasn't there when they sat down to watch *It's A Wonderful Life* or *A Miracle on 34ᵗʰ Street*, her favourite Christmas movies.

She'd sat in her chair and ate pecan pie and ice cream, while Kate and Ian talked about the menu for Christmas dinner, but she couldn't focus on the conversation or the movies.

When Kate announced the trip to Rocke-feller Centre for Christmas Eve skating, Penny felt a moment of excitement, which somehow failed to crescendo.

She loved skating, at least watching skating, since God had granted her two left feet. Still, she enjoyed it, even if it was just an observer – though Kate promised she'd change that.

However, she felt better as she dressed – slim-fit jeans, a white shirt with a caramel-coloured sweater, which matched her boots.

She even hummed as thoughts of Mike danced through her mind when Kate said he'd be joining them. Then, just as they were walking out the door, she announced that he wouldn't be coming after all.

Penny hadn't expected to be so disap-pointed. She hadn't realised she'd wanted to see him as much as she did until she wouldn't.

As they travelled to the rink she found herself looking out the window hoping to catch a glimpse of him, though she knew it was unlikely. Ian said he'd had something impor-tant to do. She wondered what could be so important, but scolded herself for the thought.

Mike wasn't her boyfriend. He could do

whatever he liked. He was a grown man. A handsome man. With a voice she couldn't shake and eyes that pierced her soul.

God help her, what was happening?

At the rink, Penny had attempted to remain the polite observer, but Kate wasn't having it. After several laps with Ian, she sought him out, determined to get her on her feet and around the rink.

Ian settled in for what was sure to be an amusing display, leaning against the side for the best vantage point. His determined wife had established that she needed no help and he would happily oblige. He loved her tenacity, even when he knew he'd eventually have to step in.

Kate's efforts to school Penny in the art of ice skating were more amusing than could've been predicted. They huffed and puffed, groaned and teetered as Kate tried to support Penny's taller frame while leading her.

Penny's feet spread wide while her knees folded in one moment, then slid in front and behind like scissors the next, while Kate clamoured to keep her upright. Ian folded over with laughter, the fountain illumining his white sweater in blue, purple and orange light.

However, his laughter halted at Kate's exclamation. She'd lost hold of Penny, who was stumbling backwards. He watched powerless, as her feet slid out from under her and flew into the air. Squinting, he anticipated her connection with the ice.

Mortification had settled in long before her feet left the ground.

The second Kate's face began to slip away, Penny knew she was about to take an embarrassing spill. She squeezed her eyes shut awaiting the impact that didn't come.

Then, as if out of nowhere, strong hands gripped her beneath the arms, holding her up, saving her.

"Falling for me, are you?" Mike's smiling face appeared beside hers, his chin nestled in the crook of her neck.

Their warm breaths mingled in the air before them as Penny's heart hammered in her chest.

He's here. She found herself smiling.

"I thought you weren't coming," she managed as he set her aright, turning her to face him.

"Thought I'd surprise you," he smirked. "Looks like you were attempting to skate."

"Kate was making me. I'm awful and she knows it." Her cheeks flushed.

"Let me."

Her eyes widened in refusal, but the words never had a chance to be uttered. Before she could think, Mike's arm was wrapped around her waist, his hand holding hers for stability while the other rested gently against her stomach, as his body fell into line with hers.

"First trick. Find your centre," he

instructed, eyes fixed upon her. The intensity of his gaze caused something in her stomach to flutter. Her heart stuttered as his fingers splayed beneath her ribcage, his grip tightening slightly as he told her to slide her right foot forward slowly.

"That's it," he encouraged.

She wobbled.

"Don't worry, I have you," he added as she squeezed his hand. "Now the left." He smiled. "Good, now the right again."

Penny hardly noticed as they moved away from the side of the rink, where Kate and Ian watched silently. Her mind was otherwise engaged.

Mike was so close.

She could smell his cologne. It was strong but not overwhelming, much like his grip – firm but gentle, cradling her against his body. She'd never paid attention to how strong he was before. She could feel the curve of his bicep against her back, the solidness of his chest where her arm rested against it, even from under his coat.

She swallowed hard, her face flushing as she took a deep breath.

"Penny…" he said her name and she felt her skin tingle. She liked the way it sounded on his lips.

This was all confusing. The feelings were strange after so long.

"Penny?" he repeated.

"Sorry?"

"I asked if you'd like to have dinner with me tonight," he chuckled at her confusion.

She nodded, unable to reply. His face was right there. All she could see was the curve of his mouth, the way the right side rose slightly higher than the left. How the white lights in the trees reflected like crystals in his eyes.

"I'd love to," she fumbled for words.

"Great. I made a reservation."

The corners of her eyes wrinkled at the announcement. "You planned this?"

"Let's just say I hoped," he replied, gently turning her to face him, their bodies flush. "I was a boy scout. They taught me to always be prepared," he smirked.

"You were a pretty good scout weren't you," her voice trembled.

"Very good."

CHAPTER 11

ew sights could compare to the view from the deck of The River Café.

Situated at the base of the Brooklyn Bridge, with the Manhattan skyline canvassed before you, it was a truly stunning view, especially tonight.

Every building was illuminated against a wintery backdrop, each light in the window like a star in the sky, framed by the frosted corners of the restaurant's large windows – it was beautiful, romantic.

When he'd made the reservation it was with one hope – that she would agree. It had taken some name-dropping and string-pulling to get a private table on Christmas Eve at such short notice, but thankfully his work connections had paid off.

Still, it had been a bold move, but necessary.

He didn't want to go too fast and push her when she wasn't ready, after all she'd been through, but he didn't have that much time.

Tomorrow was Christmas and two days after that she'd be returning to London. All he had was now.

Mike had never been a shy man. He was never one to rush either or be ruled by emotion.

But with Penny, he simply didn't know how to be. Ever since their carriage ride, where he'd told her things he'd never imagined sharing with someone he'd known only a short time, something inside him had changed.

But last night's conversation, and the promise that there could be something more between them, that the pull that yanked at that deep place in his soul, that yearned each time he saw her, could be answered – he couldn't let it go.

He couldn't let her go without at least trying. For reasons he didn't know and didn't care to have explained, he wanted to show all of him.

Everything he'd never done, he wanted to do. He wanted to heal the hurt she still felt, to soothe the pain of her loss, to open her up again. He wanted to peer inside that precious place she'd closed off, the place that cried to be freed each time she smiled, forgetting the past – the place he could lose himself in – or find himself.

Now, seated with her at their table for two, overlooking the black glass of the East River, the lights of Manhattan reflected upon it, their dinner done, he felt bold.

Reaching out his hand, he placed them atop her fingers, watching her face for her reaction. When it came, it lit up someplace deep in his stomach. Her smile was the most beautiful he'd ever seen, lighting up her face and echoing in her eyes. He could see there was still some fear, that this was all strange, almost new to her, but he wasn't deterred.

"I'm glad you came," he smiled, to ease her concerns.

"So am I." Her fingers closed around his.

"This place is amazing, and the view is

just..." She looked out, trying to find words to describe it. "It deserves to have poems written about it or something. I don't have words that could do it justice."

"I know you didn't want to come to New York for Christmas, but I hope your view of things has changed. At least a little."

"I didn't want to come. If it weren't for Kate being who she is, I definitely wouldn't have, but I'm happy I did. It's been too long since I've seen her or Ian. And Toby. He's a different child since I last saw him. It's like the world moved forward and I got left behind, but being here, in this city, with all of you, has made me see what I've been missing."

He stroked the back of her hand with his palm, urging her to continue.

"Christmas was always my favourite time of year. A time I looked forward to despite my circumstances. Kate's family became my family and each year was something I cherished. When I met Tim, and we started having Christmases together, it was like having my own family. When I lost him, I felt as if I lost everything I'd ever hoped for."

Her eyes glistened, and though every reflex

wanted to tell her not to go to that place, he knew she had to.

"Everyone told me that things would get better after he died. But none of them had ever lost someone they loved. No one could understand."

He inhaled as she did, needing that calming breath as much as she did. Her heart was beautiful, even through the pain.

"Then there was you," she continued. "You were the first person I felt understood – that I wasn't alone with those feelings – that there was someone who got it. Me." Her heart quickened as the words flowed free.

"I don't know what it is I'm feeling right now." She squeezed his hand tighter. "This is like a dream, that I don't want to wake up from, and it's scary. I barely know you, but somehow it feels...it feels –"

"Like something you can't explain, but don't want to let go of."

Penny stilled, his words reverberating in her mind.

How could he know what she felt? In the past few days, the more she thought of him, spoke to him, saw him, something had changed inside her.

Some lock that had been rusted, had been broken off, the door opened. She hadn't laughed this much in years. Felt this much in years.

And though it was frightening, though her every sinew told her to run back into that little room where she'd been hiding, protecting herself, for the past three years, there was the part of her that screamed to hold on to what she was feeling now.

Not to let it go. Not to run away but towards. She didn't know which was more terrifying – the dark, or his light, and the possibility of losing again.

She couldn't breathe.

"Penny, I know what you're feeling right now. I can see it in your eyes." He took a deep breath. "I know it's scary to feel. When I was younger, after my brother's death, I didn't want to feel. I couldn't feel it. I tried for a long time to hide. To stay buried. Low to the ground. Alone. But Ian helped me to find my way. He was my friend and encouraged me, and the first time I saw you, I saw something of me in you. I saw the person who didn't want to be seen, who wanted to shy away. That day I reached out hoping to help this beautiful woman I didn't know, not knowing what you were going through, not understanding that you were going through what I had. But even after you tore my ego in two," he smiled. "I couldn't forget you. And now I've had the chance to know you a little. I can't forget you."

Be bold. You only have two days.

"What I'm saying is … I like you. A lot. And it doesn't make sense. But does it have to?"

She was still there. She hadn't run. It spurred him on, even though his words might very well be burying him in her silence. He couldn't stop now. Finally, he said it.

"Let me make this Christmas one to remember."

CHAPTER 12

*T*here were snowflakes dancing on the buildings.

A cathedral of lights of pale blue and white, welcoming you through ornate light gates. A diva on a cloud above a Taj Mahal with a disco ball roof. Ice castles behind shop windows, illuminated in purple and pink. A tiny sparkling penguin riding upon a glittering white Lexus. Then there was the reindeer, pulling a sleigh full of robin's egg blue and white-ribboned boxes of varying sizes, large jewelled brooches tucked in between.

Her night with Mike hadn't ended as a typical date would.

There was no dinner and straight back to the house, but a walk along 5th Avenue, which was a carnival of lights in the middle of the city.

They looked into each window as they shared a bag of roasted chestnuts, purchased from a street vendor dressed as an elf. Penny had even gotten a free elf hat out of the encounter, when he heard it was a very special Christmas for her – thanks to Mike, of course.

Their gander down the avenue had taken longer than expected, as Penny took her time to admire the hard-work that had been put in to the Christmas windows, and the warm, happy feeling that seemed to emanate from every pane, sucking you into the merriment of the holiday season.

She'd understood then when so many people wanted to be in New York for the holidays. It was like nothing that could be compared to any experience she'd had before.

By the time they got in at two in the morning, with fingers intertwined, she was thoroughly tired but exceptionally happy.

He hadn't pressed for a kiss. She wasn't sure

she was ready for it, but she did grace his cheek with a peck before wishing him goodnight.

It was every woman's dream evening, and even in her sleep, Penny smiled at the memory of it.

"Merry Christmas!"

A shout started her awake as a slender body pounced onto the bed beside her.

"What?!" Penny exclaimed, utterly confused.

Kate smiled beside her, a Santa hat on her head and red pyjamas on. "Merry Christmas sleepyhead! You were taking too long to get up so I decided to speed you along." She smirked. "Must have been a good night with Mike. I waited up until one before I headed to bed, and you weren't in yet." She looked like the Grinch, the way her smile consumed her entire face.

Penny promptly hid her head beneath the sheets. "Still sleeping. Come back later." She batted her away.

"Nope. Wake up. It's after ten and you need to help Mike and Ian with dinner." She yanked the comforter from Penny's head, ruffling her hair. She moaned in response. "Now come on! The faster you get up, the faster we eat and the faster we get to presents!"

Kate had always been a Christmas Day pixie, flitting here and there, enchanted by every bit of finery she could find. It was utterly endearing and completely annoying all at the same time – especially when all you wanted to do was sleep.

It took almost half an hour for Penny to emerge from her bedroom, but once she did she was greeted by the sight of Mike, casually dressed in dark jeans and a t-shirt with Frosty the Snowman on it, chopping away at some unfamiliar vegetable.

"Good morning," he greeted her as he tried to suppress a smirk. "You can start over here by me." He tapped the chopping board with his knife, beckoning her.

"What are we doing?" she asked, peering over his shoulder curiously, looking at the piles of different vegetables and spices that enveloped the counter.

Ian was near the oven inspecting a large turkey.

"You and I are dealing with veggies and side dishes. We've got seasoned potatoes, asparagus, candied yams, Brussels sprouts and wild rice on our menu today. Ian's handling the turkey, cranberry sauce, stuffing and everything else. He picked up dessert yesterday, so we've got cherry almond cheesecake, a Yule log and some macaroons."

Penny was dumbfounded. "All that for just the four of us?"

"Not four of us," Kate piped in as she folded napkins on the dining room table. Toby was playing in his playpen quietly. "Our parents usually join us, but this year mine are in Jamaica, so it's just going to be seven of us." She looked up from her work, the grin she'd had early still painted on her face. "We always go big, just like back home. Remember?"

She did.

Christmas was always a production, with the performance happening at the dinner table. Penny always preferred the pres-how cooking in the kitchen, however, and spent most of the day there helping out. She rolled up the sleeves of her lavender cardigan.

"Let's get going."

BING CROSBY WAS CROONING 'A Marshmallow World' as they settled in around the tree. Anna and Peter, Ian's parents, were seated together on the couch.

Anna was drinking eggnog that she'd brought with her, while Peter and Ian discussed plans for a New Year's football game.

Kate was situated right under the tree with Toby, who was pulling at a silver candy cane ornament.

Mike was packing away the last of dinner. Penny had offered to help but he'd refused, telling her to enjoy herself.

And she had.

She played with her godson, watching him laugh and try to call her 'Auntie Penny' which came out as 'Annie Peeny', which only made her laugh. It was a bit like being a foster child again, surrounded by people she cared for, and who cared for her.

"Gather around everyone. Time for presents!" Kate proclaimed, holding up a large box. Toby clapped.

They each took turns exchanging gifts, cooing and giggling as they unravelled each in turn, showing them off.

Finally, it was Penny's turn. First, she gave

Toby his gift, followed by Kate and Ian. She hadn't planned for Anna and Peter, so their consolation was a large hug each. Finally, there was Mike.

She'd hesitated on whether to get him anything or not, but finally, she'd decided that she would. She pulled out the envelope and handed it over to him, their fingers brushing in the exchange, sending a ripple through her stomach.

He had once again found himself beside her on the floor. The card inside was simple, a note to wish him a merry Christmas, bought the evening after their carriage ride. A thank you for the wonderful day. She hadn't expected there would be more to add only days later, or that she'd find herself wishing she had something more to give him.

"It's just something small," she explained as he opened it, nervousness causing her stomach to turn.

"Thank you," Mike replied with a smile. "I have something for you," he whispered, concealing his words from the curious ears in the room. "It isn't here though. Meet me tomorrow?"

Penny was perplexed, but more so, she was curious. What could he possibly have for her that would need for them to meet?

"You keep surprising me."

"I know," he smirked.

CHAPTER 13

*A*nother night of thinking of him.

This time was different, however.

Penny kept being plagued by thoughts of returning home tomorrow, her dream self running from the plane that was to whisk her back to her life.

She woke breathless and even more confused. What did it mean? Her life was in London. Everything she cared about was there. Everything she wanted.

Wasn't it?

She only had one day to figure that out – today – tomorrow she was scheduled to board a flight, first thing.

Mike arrived around ten, and the pair spent most of the day talking, lamenting that Christmas Day was over already. Both avoided the ever-looming elephant in the room, which was her soon departure.

They left at two, for lunch at Del Frisco's Double Eagle Steakhouse, another unforgettable experience.

The restaurant boasted floor-to-ceiling windows that looked onto 6th Avenue and Rockefeller Centre.

They shared crab cakes and salad, Mike opted for steak while she had seared tuna, as their main. Lunch was long and full of even more conversation. They talked about the things they wanted in life – a home, family – a place to call their own. They had similar desires they discovered, but neither mentioned what it could mean.

By the time they left it was dark.

As they walked, Penny got the distinct feeling that Mike was stalling, but for what she couldn't imagine. They walked 5th Avenue again, and she was once more in awe of the lights and displays. She still wasn't sure where they were headed, and honestly, she wasn't bothered.

She was having fun and she was going to enjoy it while it lasted.

"What's this?" she asked as they arrived at Radio City Music Hall.

"This," he smirked, "is where we're going."

"The Rockettes? We're going to see the Rockettes?" Her voice was several octaves higher than normal, and her smile brilliant.

Mike offered his arm, hooking Penny's into it. "Let's see the show."

The choir sang a medley in harmony and the orchestra played as the curtain rose, illuminated in twinkling white lights. Then came the first act, a wintery night complete with a full moon, glowing white trees and of course the highlight, the dancing Rockette reindeer and a singing Santa. She shook his hand as the jolly soul came into the crowd to greet them. She was mesmerised, and it only grew the longer they watched.

Mike loved this show, it was one his uncle had taken him to several times as a child. He knew Penny would love it. And while the audience watched the show, he watched her. The way she looked on in wonder, the way her smile lit up her face and the lights of the stage reflected in her eyes. He smiled, only because he knew she was enjoying it. He tried to settle in to do the same, but his eyes kept drifting back to her.

CHAPTER 14

*T*he snow fell lightly as they walked towards Rockefeller.

"Are we going skating again?" Penny asked, a rush in her veins at the prospect.

"Not this time. In fact I'm going to need you to put this on." He pulled out a silk handkerchief. Penny looked at him puzzled. "Trust me."

She turned and allowed him to blindfold her. The next thing she felt was him leading her, and the distinct sensation of rising. They had to be on an elevator.

The chime as they reached their floor confirmed it. Then she was walking again, gripping Mike's hand to keep her wits about her.

CHRISTMAS IN NEW YORK

"Now," she felt the knot behind her head loosen. "Look."

Stunning.

Penny's lips parted as she took the sight before her, all of Manhattan lay at her feet, twinkling brightly.

Central Park looked like a frozen tundra from there, the white of the snow almost over-powering the dark of the trees.

She felt as if she were in another world, a happier place with happier people, at least for that moment.

Then she realised they were alone. At the Top of the Rock observation tower.

"Where is everyone?"

"It's just us."

"How –"

"I have my ways."

She smiled, trying to contain the emotions welling inside her. She'd never had anyone do something this amazing for her before. She looked out over the city and then back to Mike, as she tried to decipher what she was feeling.

"Mike, you've made this trip amazing. I've seen and done more now than any other before. Now this. I can't begin to thank you."

He took hold of her hand. "Say you'll come back."

"I don't even want to go." The words struck her as she uttered them, the first time she'd said them aloud, admitted what she felt.

He squeezed her hand gently, pulling her closer.

"Looking out here, seeing everything ... it's like there's a world I could be part of. A world I can't find back in London Everything I had, except for my work, I lost three years ago. I've been holding on to those memories for so long, that I stopped making new ones."

She smiled and turned to him.

"You helped me make new ones, so I guess you did keep your word. This really was a fairytale Christmas."

"So don't go."

"I have to."

"No, you don't," he breathed deeply. "Kate would love nothing more than to have you move here. So would I. You said it yourself, there is nothing but your work in London. But you could also work here. You would have family and friends here." He stepped closer.

"You can have the life you want, Penny. All you have to do is be open to it."

His proximity was doing things to her heart, making it race, and her stomach flutter. She listened to his words, each one delving deeper and deeper inside her, to the place that wanted all he was offering.

As his face closed the space between them, her eyes focused only on his lips, she knew if she did this there was no going back. If she kissed him, she couldn't go back to nothing. Couldn't let all of this just be memories. She'd want more.

Then their lips met.

Cautious at first, Mike allowed her to decide whether she wanted him to continue. When she responded, her fingers curling into the chest of his jacket, he was filled with hope that spilt over.

He wrapped his arms around her, pulling her flush against him, as his lips knew her better, the taste of her mouth sweet. She did the same, grazing his bottom lip with her tongue before exploring his taste in return.

Both mingled, each growing increasingly

MELISSA HILL

more breathless as the kiss continued. It was dizzying.

When Mike finally broke away, not wanting to push her too far too fast, his pupils were wide with the thrill of their kiss. He licked his lips as Penny's head rested against his chest, her soft breaths filling the air around him, her heart beating in tune with his.

"I don't know how to do this ... " she whispered.

"You don't have to do it alone. I'll help you figure it - *everything* - out." He pulled her close again. She lifted her head, looking into his eyes. "Say the words, and I promise I will be right there, every step of the way."

Mike fought the urge to kiss her again, his jaw clenching as he waited for her response.

She pressed her head to his chest and tried to breathe.

It was a big decision, which would change her life utterly if she made it.

Could she make such a choice?

She raised her head, determination in her eyes, and kissed him. He needed no encouragement. Her words were barely audible over the sound of his pulse in his ears, as they melted

88

between their lips. "I think I know what I want."

He pressed his smile against her lips.

Finally, they parted, and Mike turned her to the city's skyline, Penny's back pressed against his chest, as his arms wound around her.

They both looked out on the twinkling, snow-covered city, the future unknown, but their shared hopes were as bright as the scene that lay before them.

"Merry Christmas," he whispered softly.

And for Penny, for the first time in a very long time, it truly was.

MAGIC IN MANHATTAN

CHAPTER 1

*A*lice ambled through Central Park. She could feel the snow on the end of her tongue, and for the first time in weeks believed that things were beginning to get easier.

It was about time.

Harry had died in October. It had been six weeks from the diagnosis to the funeral. The apartment that they had spent two years setting up on the Upper East Side had not even been lived in.

She had stayed there last night for the first time in the master bedroom, the one that Harry had painted a pretty tortoiseshell green.

She could remember each and every one

of the items in that bedroom and the discussions and arguments they had had about them all.

She felt closer to him there, but the pain lay in her chest like a physical lump.

It hurt so, so bad.

The snow in the park was getting heavier, but instead of heading home she sat on a bench near the tree - their tree: the one where Harry had spontaneously kissed her during a walk here in the fall.

"I love you, Alice," was all he had said, but it had been enough.

The park was empty at this time of day and apart from a few kids building a snowman, no one had passed by.

Last night in the bedroom, she'd found the tickets for a concert in his best coat pocket.

It was to have been a surprise for her this Christmas. The Beatles were to play Carnegie Hall the following spring and Harry had been involved in setting up their tour.

"You've got to hear this group, they are the tops," he'd told her and he was right, the up-and-coming English band were indeed wonderful.

Just then a squirrel jumped through the snow and bounded up the tree to her left.

Alice looked up at it and realised she'd never really appreciated how beautiful the tree was. From the top, a squirrel might be able to see all the way to Staten Island. Assuming the squirrel was interested in looking.

She smiled to herself as she walked over to it.

The snow was falling harder and clinging to the bark. Alice pressed both hands into the snow, just like she and Harry had done up in the Catskill Mountains last winter.

She hugged the tree. It was nice to hug something.

As she did she noticed a small hole in the bark, one that was just large enough to fit a hand into. Alice had no idea why she did it, but she placed her hand in the hole, almost expecting to get bitten.

But instead, she felt something else entirely. She pulled out a crumpled piece of paper which she quickly realised was not just a random piece of trash, but a letter.

She went back to the bench, cleared some snow and sat down to read it.

H,

I waited for you, but once again you didn't turn up. I know I said some hurtful things for which I am sorry. I was just so scared of losing you. I don't understand why you won't leave him. If you tell him about us, we could be in London soon. This was why I wanted to see you, to tell you that the company have agreed that I should spend two years in the UK office. I said yes, because it would mean that we could be together and he would be out of our lives for good.

My heart is your heart. S xxx

ALICE WAS PLEASED to see that there was still some love out there in the world. She sometimes felt that all love and hope had died with Harry.

The world went on, life moved on.

She decided to immediately put the letter back where she had found it.

There was some lucky, (if unhappily attached) person out there waiting on it.

CHAPTER 2

*A*lice didn't return to the park for a few days.

This was going to be her first Christmas without Harry and she didn't want to spend it with her family.

So earlier that week, she took the train to Poughkeepsie to visit her sister and then after a couple of days of trying not to argue, continued on to Albany to see her mother.

By the time she got back to the city and the park, just two days before Christmas, the snow was still lying on the ground.

Alice embraced the solitude. She loved her mother but a few days had been more than enough.

She dared to visit the tree again and after looking around to make sure she wasn't being watched, she placed her hand in the hole.

This time she pulled out two pieces of paper, one was the original letter and the other was something new.

YOU ARE BEGINNING to worry me. It has now been three weeks since we last spoke and I don't think I can go on without a word from you. I think about you all day, I even dream about you. Please, please, get in touch.

S. x

THAT NIGHT when Alice got back to her apartment some of Harry's work friends came round for a visit. It was good to have company and it was even better to be able to talk about Harry properly, not the skating around the subject that her mother and sister seemed to indulge in.

However as the night wore on, her mind began to drift back to the letters.

She wondered who the couple were, how old they might be and why were they leaving notes for each other in a tree in Central Park.

Perhaps this was just a quick distraction for one of them but it seemed the other had invested significantly more in the relationship.

"More coffee?" asked Harry's oldest friend, Jim.

Alice shook her head.

"You seem to be somewhere else tonight, though I guess that's understandable," he added gently.

"I'm sorry," apologized Alice. "I've been to see my mother and travelling has taken a toll...."

"No need to say anything. I'll round up the rest of the guys and we'll let you be."

Jim was always her favourite of all Harry's pals. He understood and was sensitive.

When the apartment was all hers once more, she went to the study, the one that Harry had intended to use at weekends.

Then, not entirely sure what she was doing or why, Alice started to write a note.

I am so sorry that I have taken so long to reply. He has started to get suspicious and follows me around. I know I must tell him but please give me a few more days.

She had no idea why she was doing this. Perhaps she didn't want to let 'S' down?

Or maybe she had done it for herself

CHAPTER 3

*S*he could only hazard a guess as to when that second letter had been placed in the tree.

It might have been early morning or late at night - perhaps on the way to or from work.

So Alice took the safe option and went to the park in the early afternoon. Again, there was far fewer people around, so she removed the two letters from before and replaced it with her note.

She had to be honest and admit she was getting a thrill from all of this.

She felt excited as she crossed Columbus Circle, and as she passed several men entering the park, she wondered if any of them were 'S' on his way to the tree.

Later, Alice thought she would go back to check to see if there had been a response. She pulled out the note but she was disappointed to find it was just the one she had left.

She sat on the bench for a while, scolding herself for being so stupid, for being so childish. Then out of the corner of her eye, a figure stopped at the tree then moved on.

Alice didn't get to see the person properly but she was sure it was a man. And sure enough, when she went back to the tree her note was gone.

THE FOLLOWING MORNING the snow was beginning to melt a little so she thought she might take an early morning walk around the park.

If 'S' wasn't going to come until the afternoon, her journey would probably be fruitless.

But to her delight, there was another letter already there.

You have made me the happiest man in the world! To know you care about me and are still thinking of us being together has suddenly made me look forward to Christmas. Please tell him soon, so that we can put all of this behind us.

I love you more than I have, or will, anyone in the world. S xx

Alice knew the letter was meant for someone else but it had been written to the author of the last letter and that was her.

She sat on the bench and tears began to flow.

This girl 'H' was far luckier and richer than she possibly realised.

She decided to head back to the apartment and write a reply.

Of course I care about you.

That was all the words she felt were necessary.

Though Alice grew worried after her note had been collected but there was no response the next day or the day after that.

In fact, there was nothing for a whole week.

*T*hen on a bright snowy afternoon, when she had decided to stop being so stupid and give up this silliness altogether, she found another message.

I put your note in my wallet and took it with me to London. I have found an apartment or a flat as they call it over there, one that would be ideal for the two of us. I have to start work on January 7 but it means we could have Christmas and New Year together. Would you like that?

S. xx

Alice's heart sank. Was this all wrong? She was leading this poor man into believing, that the love of his life was going to elope across the Atlantic with him.

What if the real 'H' decided she had made a mistake? What if the real 'H placed another letter in the tree?

What then?

Alice told herself that she should just stop this whole charade now and come clean. But first, just one more note, one final message so that she could arrange to meet S and try to explain the truth about her actions.

I would love to talk with you soon so we can discuss everything. They say it is going to snow tonight so could we meet here in the park tomorrow, Christmas Eve, by this tree? There is so much I want to say to you, to explain.

SHE WENT down at the crack of dawn to place the letter in the tree to make sure S had time to reply. When she passed by later in the day, there was another note.

What a romantic idea! Of course I'll meet you by the tree. Say 1 pm and then we can go for a walk. There is so much I want to tell you as well. I will be working in London for a PR company; the same company that represents that new British group, The Beatles. There is talk that I may be working with the group directly. How exciting is that? I can't wait to see you. Until tomorrow.

CHAPTER 5

*A*lice sat most of the night looking out of her apartment window at the most exciting city in the world, her mind turning over the options.

The Manhattan skyline had never looked brighter and full of promise.

What should she do? Go to the tree? Sit on the bench and wait for the man to arrive as arranged?

S was sure to be disappointed and indeed annoyed that Alice had taken it upon herself to intercept the notes, but she'd been so taken by the romance and adventure of it all that she hadn't thought this through.

She just hoped that when she explained all this to him that he'd understand.

And perhaps the universe had meant for her to find the letter, and bring two lovelorn people together?

Clearly H, whoever she was, had no interest in being with S given that she hadn't responded to any of his notes.

Although on second thoughts, what if he became really angry? Then she'd end up feeling even worse and on Christmas Eve too. Suddenly she wondered whether going to this meeting was a good idea after all.

She sighed. Once again she wished Harry was here; he'd give her advice on the best course of action, and would know whether or not she should just let this lie or follow her instincts.

But Harry wasn't here, was he?

Alice was just getting ready to go to bed when she noticed something sitting on the bedside locker. It was the tickets to The Beatles concert that he had bought.

She smiled, realising the significance and the odd coincidence that the man she planned to meet was also connected to the group in some way.

And there and then Alice knew that her beloved was indeed pointing her in the right direction and that whatever happened at the park tomorrow was meant to be.

In fact, it didn't even matter what happened.

She was moving on, just as her husband would have wanted.

Merry Christmas, Harry.

A NEW YORK CHRISTMAS

CHAPTER 1

A New York Christmas; a lifelong dream come true.

I'd always wanted to visit the famed city, especially around Christmastime, so when the opportunity came up to visit my cousin Sarah, an estate agent who lived in Manhattan, I jumped on it immediately.

Plus the perfect opportunity to get out of Dublin for a while and nurse my broken heart.

Don, my boyfriend of two years had cheated on me just weeks before, and the fact that it happened so close to Christmas seemed to make it even harder.

Since the split I'd felt numb and broken, so

a trip to New York seemed like the ideal distraction and a perfect getaway.

It would be a reset button of sorts and while the festive atmosphere might well underscore my pain, I longed to see the legendary twinkling Christmas décor.

I wanted to feel snow crunch beneath my feet while I walked along the streets of the world-famous city.

My imagination was already alive with scenes of mesmerising department store windows and sparkling Christmas trees, Central Park, ice rinks and softly falling slow, reflecting some of my favourite Christmas movies.

To put it simply, I wanted to experience a classic New York Christmas.

Now, I sat on the sofa of Sarah's thirty-fourth-floor apartment waiting for her to come home.

She had a tall, fat Christmas tree, a real spruce. It made the entire apartment smell of fresh pine needles. Simply decorated in silver and gold, all the ornaments were replicas of antiques. Tiny red, white and black nutcracker soldiers hung from the branches with red ribbon and silver tinsel dangled, giving it a wilder aesthetic.

It was perfectly placed next to an enormous window overlooking the city streets below.

Just then my cousin burst through the front door with piles of paperwork and two laptop cases.

She was definitely one of those typical New Yorkers you hear about; the ones who always seemed to be in a hurry even when they had all the time in the world. Rushing around like they were in some sort of imaginary race.

A complete contrast to my comparatively slower-paced Dublin lifestyle.

Sarah piled her stuff on the table and then turned to me with an apologetic expression.

"Let me guess, you have to work?" I asked.

I'd only just arrived last night. I went straight to Sarah's where we had dinner - Chinese takeout — and did some catching up. That had been the extent of my New York adventures so far, but today she had promised to show me around the city and have dinner at the Russian Tea Rooms.

"Maddie I'm so sorry. If I don't get to this property right now I could lose it. Potentially a million-dollar deal or more and with Christmas only a week away I'm on a deadline. Do you hate me?" she asked.

I feigned a narrowing of my eyes but then laughed.

"Of course not. Obviously, I don't expect you to stop your life just because I'm here. Do what you would normally do. Just give me a little guidance so that I can get out and explore on my own. I'm a big girl and I can handle the Big Apple on my own. Can't I?"

Half an hour later I looked at myself in the mirror.

I took hot rollers out of my hair and brushed out the soft shoulder-length curls. Now it was thick and bouncy. My hair was a dark auburn brown and my skin was pale, typically Irish.

I put on a nice matte shade of red lipstick, not something I would normally wear but it was Christmas after all, and I was in a festive mood.

It stood out against my hair and dark lashes. I was petite at only five foot three, so I tried to always wear at least one thing that made me stand out.

It added a nice touch to my otherwise basic outfit of blue jeans and a red woollen sweater. I tugged on black calf-length leather boots, added a grey cashmere hat and saying goodbye to Sarah, headed out the door and into the bustling city.

CHAPTER 2

*M*y first stop had to be Central Park. I ambled down the street, taking it all in. The big city buzz was apparent but a lot was missing from my classic New York Christmas expectations.

For starters it was daytime, so none of the twinkling lights were on and the city had not yet been hit by its first snowfall.

It all seemed disappointingly *non*-festive so far.

Soon I came upon a massive building right across from the park. The steps were full of people sitting around eating and talking.

There were two large fir trees on either side of the entrance decorated in red velvet bows, and matching red and gold Christmas baubles, with a large gold star on top of both. Huge classical stone columns were wrapped with green ribbon that spiralled down the entire length of each.

I looked with interest at the inscription above them that read the *American Museum of Natural History.*

Of course... This place was a New York icon.

I went to a nearby street vendor and bought a piping cup of coffee and a pretzel, then joined everyone else sitting on the steps.

I was thoroughly enjoying my buttery salty snack when I got the feeling that someone was staring at me.

Before I took another bite I looked around and there, only a few feet away, was the most gorgeous man I had ever seen.

Our eyes locked and instantly I was hypnotised. I couldn't look away. He was wearing a dark wool pea coat and a well-fitted suit underneath.

His eyes were a piercing grey that changed to blue in the light. His dark hair was a bit messy, almost like the way a student would keep it and he had a layer of rugged stubble on his chin. He smiled a little at me and lifted his coffee cup in a "cheers" sort of motion. It was then that I realised I was still in a frozen state with my pretzel in the air, halfway to my mouth.

I snapped out of it and raised my cup back to him in the same manner, suddenly feeling like a messy child with butter and salt all over my mouth.

Still, he must have seen my greeting as an invite because he stood up.

He walked over and my heart immediately began to pound. Surely he would be able to hear it if he got any closer.

"Is that good?" he asked pointing to the pretzel.

"Yes, it is," I replied.

"May I?" He gestured at the space next to me on the steps.

"OK." I was completely confused. I thought New Yorkers were supposed to be impolite and unapproachable.

"Seems like it must be. The way you were eating it; it looked like you were really enjoying it."

"You were watching me eat?"

"Well, yes," he said with a grin that was childlike and made me feel like I was playing some coy game. "So how long are you in town?"

"What? How do you know I'm visiting?" I asked, with my mouth wide open.

"The way you stood in front of the building staring at it. Only folks who aren't from around here can look at it and still be in awe. The locals are so used to it that they tend to take it for granted."

"Well, it is beautiful. And yes, I am visiting. To be honest I came here for a classic Christmas with snow and festive decorations and all that. But so far this is the only building I've seen that is decorated. I haven't been here very long though," I stopped suddenly, feeling like I was rambling on.

Why was I even telling this handsome stranger my every thought?

"Well, maybe you just need someone to show you around. A classic New York Christmas is out there; you just have to know where to go," he added gently. "Happy to point you in the right direction if you'd like."

There was a long pause. I stared at him. Looking into his sparkling grey eyes and then at his soft lips.

"I think I would - like that, I mean."

"Great. I'm Blake by the way." He reached a hand out to shake mine.

'Madeleine.'

"Shall we get started then? There's something inside I want to show you," Blake said as he stood up.

I followed him up the steps to the museum and threw away the last of my pretzel and empty cup into a nearby bin.

He led me inside the lobby, and there right in the middle of the huge open space was one of the quirkiest Christmas trees I had ever seen. It was full of paper ornaments. Origami ornaments.

"This is how we kick off the holiday season at the museum. It's been going on for almost thirty years now. "

"It's beautiful," I said as I went in for a closer

look. There were all sorts of animal decorations, from turtles to zebras … all made of the most delicate paper. Some were shiny and others were matte, but they were all expertly done.

"There must be hundreds," I said in awe.

"About five hundred in all," he said, and then added. "So you like it?"

"Like? I love it."

"Good. Then I am off to a good start," he grinned. "Next up my office," he said as he walked off further into the museum.

"Office?"

"Yes, I work here."

Now the messy mad scientist hair and wool pea coat made sense. He definitely looked the part. I scurried after him to catch up.

Soon we arrived at a door labeled 'museum staff only.' Blake used a key card to unlock the door and we stepped into a quiet long hallway.

"This way."

"Where are you taking me?" I asked, a little unnerved and wondering if I really should be trusting this random New York stranger.

He laughed and said, "I swear, it's just my

office. I know it's a bit creepy in this part of the building but trust me."

Somehow I did trust him. I can't explain it, but for some reason, it felt like we had known each other for a long time even though we had only just met.

We came to a vast staircase and climbed two or three flights before finally reaching a hallway with people moving in and out of offices.

Blake showed me into his, and as soon as I stepped in I immediately fell in love with it. The wood was dark and heavy and a massive bookcase filled with old books covered an entire wall.

There was a heavy oak desk in the middle that had piles of papers and specimens in glass jars. A proper mad scientist's office.

He went over to the large windows. "Come and have a look."

What other surprise could this intriguing stranger have in store for me? When I got to the window I looked down. From this point, you could see almost all of Central Park.

"This is your view? It's amazing. You are so lucky."

"I know. It's good, right? Especially when it's snowing."

I looked at him. Who was this man? This was wonderful; more than I expected from anyone, let alone a stranger.

He must have seen the questioning look in my eyes because he caught my gaze and held it.

The chemistry between us was so thick it filled the room.

I barely knew this man, had only been in his company for thirty minutes at the most.

What was happening to me?

I was in a historic New York building with the vastness of Central Park below us. Blake leaned in closer his voice down to a whisper and said, "Want to get closer?"

"Closer to what?" I stepped backwards a little, suddenly afraid he was able to read my thoughts.

"To the park of course."

"Oh, yes of course. I'd love to."

"Okay. But first, we need to make a pit stop." He led the way out the door and back down into the main building.

A pit-stop? I was intrigued afresh, but this

man was full of surprises. I liked being surprised so I didn't ask.

Outside, he walked down the museum's front steps and I followed closely behind, noticing that dusk was approaching. "How about we grab some food and have a picnic in the park?"

"That sounds like a perfect idea."

"Great," He led the way to a row of street vendors, got one of everything and made us a sort of street food buffet — pizza slices, a gyro, hot dogs, a couple of bottled waters, and two hot chocolates.

We entered the park and the beauty of it took my breath away. Most of the trees had lost their leaves and their spiralling bare branches reached high into the sky.

I understood how people could stroll the entire length of this massive space daily.

We sat down on a grassy area near a long avenue of trees. Blake laid out our buffet in front of us.

"That's a lot of food," I joked.

"Yes, well I couldn't decide what your first New York food vendor experience should be, so I got them all.

"Try the pizza first. You have to fold it like this," he said as he picked up a slice and folded it before handing it to me.

I laughed a little and took a bite from the cheesy gooeyness, while he did the same with the other slice.

"Delicious!" I cried after I swallowed my first bite.

"And that's not even the best pizza in town. Okay for a street vendor, but by far not the best. I'm glad you are pleased though."

Before long I was stuffed. I lay down on the grass looking up at the trees to give my full stomach some room to digest. He did the same.

"I am so full," I said.

"Yes, me too," he said.

"We're both full of New York," he joked. I laughed and then he joined in.

Then while we were both laughing and in good spirits, the loveliest thing happened.

CHAPTER 5

While we'd sat chatting on the grass, it had gradually darkened into early evening.

The sky was still a light pink from the setting sun, but also dark blue from the oncoming night. But right then, as if out of nowhere and without ceremony, some of the nearby trees lit up.

Sitting up immediately I gasped.

"That's incredible … so beautiful."

I looked around and it seemed like the entire park came to life with twinkling lights.

The bare trees all around were decorated with delicate hanging bulb strands. It was so beautiful it almost brought me to tears.

I took it all in, absorbing the magic.

Now it truly felt like Christmas.

I looked at Blake, but he wasn't looking at the lights, he was looking at me. His face was lit from the glow of the nearby trees and I got the feeling he had been watching my reaction the entire time.

"I can't believe this is real," I said.

"Me neither," he replied gently, and again I got the feeling he wasn't talking about the lights.

Then he looked me directly in the eye and leaned in a little closer.

"Madeline, I don't normally do this. Meet a stranger on the steps and take off and spend an afternoon with them. It's been really special, and unusual for me. I just thought I should say something to give you a little insight as to who I am. It's as if I can't separate myself from you…"

My eyes got wide. I had never had a man be so forthright with me. To just put his cards on the table like that. Things like this just didn't happen. At least, not outside of the movies.

Was this guy playing games with me? Did he have something else in mind? Was that statement about not wanting to separate from me just a ploy to get me back to his place or something?

My warmed heart was beginning to turn a little cooler and now I felt very naive.

"I've said too much, I can tell I've made you uncomfortable," he said.

Yet, he had done nothing to make me not trust him, I realised. I was the one planting these negative thoughts in my head. I had only just met him and I was already assuming the worst. The break-up had done a number on me. The experience of being cheated on had scared me more than I had known. I willed myself to stop all the chatter in my head and to just stay in the moment.

"No, I'm fine. I'm sorry, I'm just not used to such honesty," I admitted.

"Right, it was a bit too much. I'm sorry I don't know where that came from."

The awkwardness was broken and everything was well again.

"Let's take a closer look," I said as I stood up. I made my way to the trees and the closer I got the more I realised just how many tiny lights there were.

They twinkled and glowed in the fading daylight. Now, it was beginning to look and feel a lot more like A New York Christmas.

This was that festive magic I had expected from the city. It was all so lovely. My feelings of paranoia and lack of trust began to melt away. The season had that effect on people I supposed.

It made them softer, more trusting, and more open. It was affecting me in that way now. The lights made Blake's eyes now seem a crystal watery grey. Like the sea during a storm.

"I want to show you more; more of the city's festivity, if you'll let me," he said.

"I would love that."

He arched his elbow out and I duly wrapped my arm under his. He then led me down the path.

"Where are we going now?"

"It's a surprise. But I think you will like it."

I grinned. This guy seemed to like surprising me, and I loved being surprised.

I wondered what next he had in store.

$\mathcal{W}$e strolled through the park arm in arm, and chatted more about our lives.

Blake told me about his work and what he did at the museum. "I was actually just taking a break from finishing a paper when I was sitting on the steps earlier. I had planned to go back inside and finish. Then I saw you."

"Oh, no I'm so sorry. Had I known I would not have let you stop working for this." I said, feeling guilty.

"It was worth it. I had to take that chance when I saw it. I would forever regret it if I didn't."

My heart fluttered into my throat. His

honesty was so disconcerting, yet refreshing too.

He never hesitated; he just blurted out what he was thinking, and I admired that.

Finally we emerged from the park onto Fifth Avenue, the world-famous shopping mecca. I immediately felt a thrill of excitement when I spied the huge giant snowflake hanging above the centre of the street, signalling where we were.

"Come on, this way," Blake urged, leading me further down the avenue.

We came to an imposing building across from the park entrance and slowed our pace when arriving at the front of it. The Bergdorf Goodman department store. I looked up at the windows and squealed with delight. The festive displays were beyond words.

It was an outdoor White Christmas scene. The setting was a winter forest and mannequins wore long sequinned designer gowns in Victorian style.

They were draped in white fur capes that trailed several feet behind them. The background was full of Christmas trees and various branches and shrubs all decorated with artificial snow and glitter, which also covered the ground.

Everything was white and the light reflecting off the scene in the city darkness made the entire window glow.

Even the accessories were white, including the glittering diamond bracelets and necklaces worn by the mannequins. It was a vivid, magical wintery scene and I was completely absorbed in it, trying to take it all in.

So much so that I almost forgot I wasn't alone.

"Do you like it?" Blake asked.

"I love it! It's everything I could have hoped for. This is the exact kind of thing I longed to see," I rambled on.

Blake laughed at my enthusiasm and said, "I'm so glad. I rush by here every year and never really stop to take a closer look. I guess because in the back of my mind, I knew I wanted to share it with someone."

I looked up at him. Every second longer I spent in his company I was falling for this man, and it was scaring me. I watched him look at the window, smiling. I could stare at him forever.

"There's another great one further down the street at Saks if you want to keep going?"

My eyes widened, "Saks?" I repeated in barely a whisper.

Blake chuckled, obviously delighted by my enthusiasm. "You are too cute." Then he looped my arm in his and led me further along the busy street.

We stopped at another street vendor along the way.

"Can't go see the Saks windows without hot chocolate," he insisted.

"But I've already had one today."

"Oh, do you have a chocolate limit or something?" He joked. "It's the holidays. Enjoy yourself. And at Christmas, hot chocolate is *definitely* a New York tradition."

I laughed. "Well, I am a bit cold, and I do like traditions."

*B*lake bantered with the street vendor a little. He had that effect on people; able to talk to them like they were old friends.

We walked until we came upon the Saks building.

"Wait, hold on," he said as he put one hand over my eyes and one arm around my back to guide me.

This was adorable. He really wanted me to get the full experience. I slowly shuffled my feet as he positioned me in front of the window, then he took his hand away from my eyes and said: "Okay, open your eyes."

I did. It took me a few seconds to process

what I was seeing. In the first window was the setting of a Victorian living room, or parlour, as they must have called it then.

There was a Christmas tree in the corner of it and on the wall a sign that read, "Twas the Night Before Christmas."

Blake stood beside me and said. "It's a story, each window is a scene from the story."

My eyes watered over. This was breathtaking.

I stepped closer, completely hypnotised by it.

In the centre of the parlour was a fireplace, and 'stockings hung by the chimney with care.'

The stockings must have been true vintage pieces, with red and green patterns, not the commercial Christmas ones you get now, but actual socks.

The green garland above the fireplace was simple and thin, but also vintage in appearance. A tree was decorated with handmade orna-ments, each different from the other and made of wood or paper.

There were a few glass baubles, but not many, as it would have been a luxury to have those during that period.

A small toy train and tracks went around the bottom of the tree skirt while an old wooden vintage train set circled intricately wrapped presents with red, green, and gold paper and velvet ribbon.

There were only a few presents, maybe five in total. Large winged-back chairs were set before the fireplace with a cosy blanket throw across the back.

A small table near the chairs had an old book on it, *Twas The Night Before Christmas*.

I looked at Blake, and smiled, "It's the loveliest thing I've ever seen."

"I'm glad you like it," he said. "Come on, let's see the whole story."

"Wait," I said.

He stopped and looked back at me.

"Thank you, Blake. For all of this."

"It's my pleasure." He put his elbow out for me again and I encircled my arm in his, took a sip of my creamy hot chocolate and continued on.

The next window was the children's bedroom. They were snug in their beds and wore adorable night clothes in a wrought iron bed.

The requisite sugar plum fairies hung from the ceiling, and sprigs of holly from the corners.

The next window had a white powdered rooftop with smokey chimneys, and featuring the man himself.

There was a large sled being driven by Santa Claus, as it landed on the roof. He wore the iconic Victorian dark maroon suit, not the bright red and white one, common today.

He had rosy cheeks and a thick white beard and next to him was a large velvet bag full of intricately wrapped gifts. The reindeer were so lifelike and each one wore jingle bells.

The whole thing was pure Christmas magic.

The store really went out of its way to make this classic festive story come to life, and I was grateful to have the opportunity to see it.

"So, is it all you hoped for so far?" Blake queried.

"It's more than that. I've heard about this kind of thing and have seen pictures, but experiencing it in person doesn't compare."

"I'd love to show you more Christmassy stuff while you are in town. I wish we could keep today going for longer, but I really do have to get back to my project. Would you allow me to walk you home?"

I tried not to sound disappointed that our festive whistle-stop tour was now coming to an end.

*W*e walked back through the length of the park and at one point, Blake gently reached for my hand.

When we came to the other side and exited back onto the street, I felt like we had entered a different world.

I'd almost forgotten that I was in the city because the park had once again made me feel like I was in a fairy tale.

We finally got to Sarah's condo and stepped under the long red awning that covered the path in an archway to the front door.

"This is it," I said.

"Are you free tomorrow night?" Blake asked then. "I'd like to take you to dinner."

"Yes, I would love that," I said, hardly daring to believe it.

"Great. Pick you up here at 7?" Then he looked down at me and continued,

"Madeline, what is happening here? This is so unreal. I've never connected with anyone this instantly."

"I ...I'm not sure."

Then he leaned in and hugged me. A soft gentle hug, because the doorman was watching.

"I'll pick you up tomorrow, OK?" he whispered.

Then we parted ways. He stood there watching until I went inside, feeling like I was walking on air.

Upstairs, I opened the door to the apartment to find Sarah at the kitchen table, piles of paperwork spread out before her. She looked exhausted.

I must have been glowing because as soon as she looked up at me she raised an eyebrow.

"What happened to you? You look almost... hypnotised," she said.

I skipped over to her. "I met someone ... a guy."

"What? You've been in New York less than 24 hours and it's the holidays. How?"

We both laughed. Then I told her everything. Of how I had sat in front of the museum at lunchtime and met Blake. I explained the rest without leaving out any details. Sarah was astounded.

"Wait stop," she said. "Let's move onto the couch. I need to get away from this workspace." Then she went into the kitchen and opened a bottle of red wine and brought two glasses to the couch. "Is this guy for real? I almost feel like you made him up. No one is that perfect."

"Yes, he does seem too good to be true, so much in fact that there's a problem."

"Well, that's a relief at least," Sarah laughed.

"I can't help but think he's pulling some kind of trick or something. Maybe he's just trying to get me into bed. He's so romantic and seems so honest. Every time he says something about his feelings for me, I can't enjoy it because I feel like there's some sort of ulterior motive."

Sarah sighed and rolled her eyes. "When you said there was a problem, I thought you meant with your perfect man. But there's no problem there. Just an issue you made up in your head."

I sighed. "Maybe you're right."

"I know I am. Trust me. So, what are you going to wear to dinner tomorrow night?"

My eyes grew wide. I hadn't even thought that far ahead.

"I have no idea."

"Come on, let's see what you brought," Sarah stood up and went into the guest bedroom where I had my stuff.

We threw open the closet and I tried on every outfit I owned. It was a complete fashion show because with it being cold outside, I had to put on every outfit and then put on my coat and boots to see if everything went together.

"I don't like anything I have. I just don't have the right clothes for freezing weather," I groaned.

"Come on, I do," Sarah grabbed the wine and glasses and led me to her room.

We went through the whole thing all over again with her clothes. I tried on every dress she owned. I found a festive red one in a fitted style that went to just above my knees.

It was off the shoulder, with quarter-length sleeves and made of pure silk. This made it elegant, but not over the top; the perfect balance.

Sarah clapped her hands in delight. "That's the one. It's perfect."

CHAPTER 9

*T*he next day, while I spent a lovely morning wandering around Manhattan again, Sarah had a break for lunch so I met her at a little café near her office.

She was on her phone most of the time, still conducting business so I was kind of glad when it was over. I wanted to prepare for tonight anyway.

Around six o'clock, I began to get jitters. What if Blake didn't show up?

I took a deep breath and allowed myself to trust this man. Trust that he would show and not stand me up. I went ahead and got dressed and at seven o'clock sharp, the doorman rang up.

Blake was downstairs waiting for me. I breathed a sigh of relief, grabbed my coat and headed out.

He stood in the lobby and I was taken aback at how I felt as soon as I locked eyes with him.

He stood there, his tall figure towering in the brightly lit lobby. He wore an elegant black suit and his woollen pea coat. He topped it off with a red silk scarf around his neck, the perfect compliment to my dress.

His eyes were wide as he looked me up and down.

"Madeline, you looked stunning," he said greeting me with a light hug.

The doorman held out my coat, offering to help me put it on.

"Allow me," Blake said.

He slid my coat on and then planted a light kiss on my cheek. "Shall we?" he asked, as he offered me his arm.

A black car was waiting for us. I was confused, as I'd thought we would surely be walking.

A few minutes later, I stepped out and nearly gasped out loud. The Plaza Hotel.

A visit there would be a treat for anyone at

any time I knew, but at this time of year, it was doubly astounding.

The entrance was beautifully decorated in holly wreaths and delicate lights. It was intricate and elegant, and again had that classic New York feel I'd so longed for.

Blake put his arm around me and said, "You mentioned you wanted an old-fashioned Christmas experience. There's no better place for that than this hotel. It hasn't changed much since it was built in the early nineteen hundreds."

I looked up at him. This was perfect.

Blake flashed a grin, before putting his hand on the small of my back and leading me inside.

The lobby was alive with festive cheer, with several Christmas trees elegantly decorated and buzzing with people enjoying the holidays; everybody beautifully dressed and being fussed over by attentive waiting staff beneath sparkling chandeliers.

I was in complete awe of the glamour. I really did feel like I had stepped back in time.

Even with me in heels, Blake still towered over me. As we stood there in the lobby, surrounded by all this festive beauty, he looked down and then in one unexpected motion he kissed me.

"I'm so sorry, I couldn't help it," he said, pulling away quickly.

I didn't want him to stop, and while I loved his politeness and hesitation, I wanted to keep going.

Right then I forgot all about my ex-boyfriend and any mistrust I had in Blake. It had all vanished in just twenty-four hours.

Walking around New York, and exploring a new world was exactly the kind of thing I needed to get a different perspective of how magical life could be.

Blake and I enjoyed a silver service dinner in the Palm Court; turkey roast and vegetables with brandy and for dessert we shared pudding and a cup of nutmeg.

At the end of the night, we said our good-byes at the door of Sarah's condo, with no pressure to carry things further. Almost the way old-fashioned courting would've been.

"So, see you tomorrow night?" he suggested. "I was thinking maybe ice-skating this time."

He leaned in and planted another kiss on

my lips. Slow and romantic, full of feeling and it made me feel a bit dizzy.

It was like this man really could read my mind.

CHAPTER 10

*T*he next day I went for a daytime walk through the park by myself.

Reliving memories from the time before with Blake, I was in a great mood and I smiled and said hello to every passerby - so much so that eventually people started avoiding the crazy-looking Irish girl.

When I neared the museum I remembered the pretzel stand so I thought I would grab one.

Exiting the park, I crossed the street near the building and suddenly saw Blake sitting on the steps.

With an attractive female alongside him.

I stopped in my tracks, feeling instantly duped as realisation dawned.

Was this what he did all day? Was this his pick-up spot? Did he even work in the museum at all?

I was crestfallen but worse, my heart was breaking again.

I watched as they talked to each other. They seemed very comfortable together and smiled a lot as they chatted, very much like we had only a couple of days before.

I debated whether I should go up to him — to confront him - or should I just let it go, walk away and never talk to him again.

After a few minutes of staring and not knowing what to do, I watched as they both stood up. It was unbelievable, they were going inside.

This *was* his thing! This is what he did.

My despair quickly turned into anger, and I stomped off in their direction. I stood at the bottom of the steps as I watched them disappear into the museum together.

Just then Blake turned in the doorway. He locked eyes with me and smiled in recognition. But I didn't smile back. Instead, my eyes darted immediately to the woman and then back at him.

Turning quickly, I raced down the steps and back into the park. I wanted to disappear as soon as I could in case he was coming after me. I didn't want to hear his pathetic excuses.

I ran all the way home, in disarray. Sarah was at work and I had no one to confide in. Everything suddenly felt grey. Now the cheery Christmas tree in the living room seemed to taunt me.

CHAPTER 11

I fell asleep on the couch and woke up a few hours later.

I looked around in the darkness. It didn't look like Sarah had come home yet.

I checked the time and saw that it was only seven o'clock. It felt so much later. The embarrassment of what had happened earlier flooded back.

Why was I letting this get me down? Yes, I was hurting, but I came to New York to enjoy myself. I wasn't going to let a player destroy my dream trip.

What would I be doing right now if I'd never met Blake? I would probably be ice-skating at Rockefeller Center, under the giant tree.

It was exactly what he'd suggested we do tonight. He knew me well - or I should say he knew well how to woo idiot New York tourists like me.

I pulled myself together and decided to go anyway.

I would put all thoughts of him out of my mind and continue on as if I had never met him.

I washed my face and got changed into a comfortable pair of jeans and a sweater, perfect for ice skating, then headed downstairs to the lobby where the doorman stopped me.

"Miss," he said. "You have several messages from Mr Blake." He handed me a few small notes.

"Thank you," I said grabbing them and walking out the door.

As soon as I saw a bin on the street, I tossed them inside. I didn't open them. I didn't need to.

CHAPTER 12

Finally, I arrived at Rockefeller Plaza.

I could see the tree as I approached, but getting up close to it was beyond words.

I titled my head back staring up mesmerised at the massive spruce right in the centre of the plaza above the ice-rink.

It was even more glorious in person. There must've been a million lights on it. The entire plaza was decorated for the holiday season; beautiful life-sized angels blowing trumpets, and giant painted nutcracker soldiers lined up all round.

Below on the ice rink, people were skating and full of cheer and laughter, while spectators sipped hot chocolate and ate peppermint fudge.

I sat down on nearby bench and gazed at the tree.

Its magic now seemed to only mock my sadness. I thought of Blake again, wanting to cry.

I was only kidding myself with all these distractions. It wasn't working.

It was then, right in that moment of thinking about him that I heard a familiar voice.

"May I?"

I looked up to see Blake towering over me. He was gesturing at the space on the bench beside me.

I didn't say anything but he sat anyway.

"Madeline, I've been trying to get hold of you all day. The doorman wouldn't let me up no matter how much I pleaded with him. I tried for an hour at least," he said.

I just looked at him and while I willed my heart to harden, I could feel my eyes watering over.

His sincere way of talking was enough to make me crack. I wanted things to be as they were before. I did not trust this man. I don't think I trusted any man at this point.

"Why did you run off like that today?" he asked.

I could barely get the words out. My voice was shaking.

"I watched you, on the steps. Talking to that girl and then I saw you bring her back into the museum, just like we did. Is that what you do to pick up women? It works. It worked on me, I was stupid enough to fall for it, just like the girl today was."

Blake's eyes were wide. At first, I thought they were wide at having been caught. But then he spoke.

"Madeline, that's not what that was — at all," he gasped. "You've got it so wrong, and I'm sorry if what you saw hurt you. That's the last thing I would ever want to do, but if you would just let me explain …"

"I don't see the point in an explanation. I could never tell if you were lying."

"That is true," he said. "Would you like to meet her then?"

"Meet who?" I asked.

"The woman you saw me with earlier.

That's the only way I can prove that I'm not lying. She's at my apartment right now," he said.

"What? She's in your apartment?" I repeated outraged at his brazenness.

"Yes, I couldn't make it home for Christmas this year, so she came to the city so that I had some family around."

"Family?"

"Yes. She's my sister."

My heart sank. I couldn't say why, but I believed him.

Now I felt like a complete idiot. I was kicking myself for acting so rashly earlier.

Sarah was right. The problem wasn't this man. It was me. The breakup had left me a paranoid mess.

"I'm so sorry. I feel so stupid," I said.

"It's okay. Don't be. I'm kind of glad it happened."

"What? Why?"

"Because I wasn't sure if you felt anything for me. When we look at each other I can feel a connection, but you haven't said anything... about what you think or how you might feel. But seeing your reaction today ... now I know for sure you feel something too. And that I might be more than just your New York Christmas guide."

I sat in silence and processed what he had said. Perhaps I needed this to bring me to that next level.

This entire thing had been such a roller coaster.

"So, we're okay?"

"Yes, we're okay. And I'm sorry," I whispered, feeling stupid again.

He held my shoulders and turned me toward him.

"No need to apologise. I want you to be honest with me. I know this is crazy and we only just met, but I think we might have something here. I knew it when I saw you for the first time. You're the best Christmas present I could have asked for. Maybe this was meant to be."

I looked up at him, my eyes watering over. This dear sweet man was all I could ever hope for and he was pouring his heart out to me. Beneath the most magical Christmas tree in the world.

"Now, I seem to remember I promised you ice skating."

And when a little later Blake took my hand and led me out onto the ice rink, I looked around again at the twinkling lights on the tree and the scene around us, unable to believe that I was actually here and this was really happening.

Everything felt so surreal. And impossibly romantic - almost like something from a movie.

But then the most magical thing of all happened.

Out of nowhere, it began to snow. Small perfect snowflakes fell on our faces and we laughed amongst the beauty of it all.

This New York Christmas was perfect, even better than I had imagined, more than I could have ever dreamed of.

And as Blake leaned down and kissed me, I also knew I wanted to experience it over and over again.

A WINTER WONDERLAND

A WINTER WONDERLAND

Dakota absentmindedly turned her taxicab down Sixth Avenue.

The Avenue of the Americas as it was officially named, was bustling as always, even more so now that it was noon and many of the business executives who inhabited the sparkling glass buildings were spilling into the street in search of lunch.

Dakota turned to her co-pilot, sprawled out on the passenger seat. Scratching behind his long, fuzzy ears, she said with a sigh, "Here we go again, Thor, 'another day, another dime'."

Thor looked up at the petite blonde with his eternally sad eyes and wagged his tail.

"Here, let's adjust those silly reindeer

antlers," she said in the soothing voice she reserved for her favourite Basset hound. "I know that goofy headgear is slightly emasculating but I do think that the big red bow tied around your collar really brings out the highlights in your fur."

Thor yawned.

"The important thing is that the tourists love you. We are the epitome of all that is good and right about New York City, my friend. Where else can shoppers wind down after a long day at Macy's with a ride in a festive, holiday taxicab complete with a musically talented Basset?"

She offered him a piece of the string cheese she was nibbling on.

"Honestly, singing carols along with our passengers was one of the best ideas I've ever had. Can you believe the tips we're getting? People are actually disappointed when we get them to their destinations quickly," she said, smiling down at the dog.

Her cell phone began playing the opening notes of Beethoven's 5th Symphony. She groaned and said, "And that would be my mother calling, no doubt to remind me that I am far from home and without marital prospects as yet another Christmas season shifts into high gear."

She paused mid-rant as she angled the taxi toward a man standing on the curb, hailing her cab with a raised hand.

"I've told her a hundred times that you are the only boy for me, Thor. Who else would put up with a broke, guitar-wielding, organically grown flower child?" she went on as she allowed voicemail to answer her mother's call.

The dog thumped his tail on the seat in agreement as their latest fare opened the cab door. Dakota glanced at the preoccupied man through the steel grate that separated the front and back seats. He was good-looking with a muscular build that filled out his Armani suit nicely.

This job has its perks, she thought to herself.

"Where to?"' she asked, aloud.

"Katz's Deli on East Houston," he answered as he placed his briefcase on the seat beside him. He looked up and found himself face-to-face with the hound that had hoisted his antlered head onto the back of the seat and let it rest, smashed against the grate.

The man's sudden start and subsequent burst of laughter frightened Thor who bayed loudly and jumped back down into the front seat.

"Hey, quit harassing my ferocious guard dog," Dakota said in mock sternness. "Now that you've frightened him, he probably won't sing Christmas songs with you."

For the first time, the man looked about the festively decorated cab, heard the holiday soundtrack and looked into the rear-view mirror at the smiling, violet-blue eyes of the cab driver.

He smiled, "I regret to inform your dog that I don't sing."

"It's required of everyone who rides in this cab, mister," she chided, "Now pick a song or Thor will do it for you."

"You didn't let me finish," he responded. "I was going to say that I don't sing with *strangers*."

He then bowed slightly and said, "Allow me to introduce myself. My name is Nick Marshall."

Dakota caught his eye in the mirror, grinned and replied, "Pleased to meet you, Mr. Marshall. I am Dakota Raine. And yes, that is my legal name," she said before he could ask. "It's a slightly awkward reference to the location and weather conditions at the time of my conception. If you guessed that my parents were into protests, pot and free love, you would be correct."

She turned up the volume on the all-Christmas-music-all-the-time radio station.

"OK, now that we are properly acquainted, let's hear it," Dakota said encouragingly.

"I have to warn you that I possess a limited vocal range," he hedged. "Some people might even say my voice is uncommonly flat."

"I'll be the judge of that," she told him as she further cranked up the volume.

Together the cab's occupants joined Andy Williams who was crooning, *Sleigh bells ring, are you listening?*

Dakota pulled the cab to the curb in front of Katz's as the trio howled and sang their way through the song's final notes, "...walkin' in a winter wonderland!"

Dakota was laughing as she told him, "Whoever suggested that you lack musical talent knew what he was talking about."

"You can't say I didn't warn you," he declared as he opened the door and stepped out. He held out his fare and a generous tip through her open window. Fat, heavy snowflakes had started to fall from the grey December sky.

"Thanks for the lift. You and your dog are two in a million," said a grinning Nick Marshall. Although he couldn't sing, his voice gave her goosebumps just the same.

Trying not to blush, Dakota responded, "You'd better hurry inside, your hair is turning white."

He brushed the snow off of his head and said, "Hey, if you're looking for a fare around seven-thirty tonight, I could use a lift home."

"I'm sorry," she told him. "Honestly, I'd love to but I have a date ...."

He smiled to hide his disappointment. "I should have known that a lady as lovely as yourself would have a full social calendar."

She shook her head and smiled back. "Not that kind of date. I'll be playing my own crazy mix of indie-soul music over at Think Coffee in the West Village," she told him just as a car horn started blaring behind her. "Oops, gotta go! I'm double parked. It was great carolling with you," she hollered out the window as she reluctantly pulled away.

* * *

Later near midnight, Dakota was saying good-night to an appreciative coffee house audience. As she turned to grab her guitar case stashed behind the stage, a deep voice from behind her asked, "What? No back-up singer tonight?"

Dakota looked up into Nick Marshall's smiling face. She feigned indignation and responded, "No dogs allowed. Something about 'health code violations'. Can you believe it?"

"Most distressing," he agreed and continued, "I'd offer to buy you a cup of coffee but this place appears to be closing. Care to join me for a sandwich at the bar down the street?"

"Perfect timing," she answered, grabbing her guitar case. "I'm starving."

They walked unhurried down the street. The late-night date continued into the early morning as they sat across from each other at a window booth, enjoying wine and conversation.

"So, you still haven't told me, Ms Raine, what brought you from Iowa to the Big Apple?" Nick asked.

Dakota shrugged and looked at snow falling outside the window, glittering in the dim bar light.

"This probably sounds corny," she said turning her violet-blue eyes to meet his gaze. "I came here to make a difference with my music. I've been writing and singing ever since I can remember and there's nothing that can describe the feeling I get when I make a connection with another person through a song. The right lyrics at the right time can strip people down to their bare souls, you know?"

She looked at him earnestly, wondering if she had bared too much of her soul to this man she had met only hours ago.

He reached for her hand. "Dakota Raine, you *do* have a gift for moving people with your music," he told her. "Look, I am not a spontaneous man. I start each day with a plan of action which I always execute fully before I allow myself to sleep at night. I have a phone stuck to my ear 24/7 because I like to think I am important and in demand." He continued, still holding her gaze, "I do not sing of snowmen and Parson Brown with cabbies and their hounds. And I most definitely do not hang out in coffee houses hoping to get a date with the girl with the guitar even if she does happen to be gorgeous."

She held her breath as he stopped to catch his.

"But here I am just the same, shirking responsibilities to sit in a semi-seedy joint in the wee hours of the morning hoping a little of your magic will rub off on me."

Dakota stood as she reached across the table to take his face in her hands. She closed her eyes and gave him a long, sweet kiss. He smelled of Vintage Black cologne and tasted of the fruity Merlot they had been sharing.

She pulled away reluctantly and sat back down.

"So now what, Mr Marshall?" she asked.

He took a deep breath and answered, "Now I drive you home so *I* can go and contrive a means to sweep you off your feet tomorrow night," he replied firmly.

"I can't wait to see what to see what tomorrow brings," she smiled.

* * *

Less than 24 hours later, during the final notes of her last set, Dakota once again anxiously scanned the faces in the crowded coffee shop. But the one person she hoped to see remained disappointingly absent.

Suddenly, she knew the whole thing had been too much like one of those silly chick flicks that she loved to watch but would never admit to enjoying.

She looked down at her cream-colored peasant blouse and her embroidered, flowing skirt as she flushed with anger and embarrassment. Had she really believed that a high society, Armani suit-wearing businessman would leave behind the skyscraper world for a carolling cab driver?

"You're working in a *coffee* house, Dakota," she reminded herself between clenched teeth, "Time to wake up and smell it. The sophisticated Nick Marshalls of this world are but briefly amused by the earthy Dakota Raines."

She shut her guitar case. "What were you thinking?" she said aloud as she picked up the case. Then she quickly grabbed her coat and stuffed it under her free arm, unconcerned about protecting herself from the snowy wind that had been gusting all day between the tall buildings.

Dakota hurried past the small crowd of fans who had gathered to thank her for the night's music. She pushed open the coffee shop door and slammed directly into a broad chest.

"I'll spare you the, 'we've got to stop running into each other like this' line," Nick said steadying her gently with his hands on her shoulders. "I'm so disappointed that I couldn't be here earlier to listen to your beautiful voice, but I was delayed while attempting to persuade a white stallion to work past his quitting time."

Dakota's mind was swirling. Two minutes ago she had been dismissing him and now here he was, as promised, taking her breath away with his good looks, his Vintage Black smell and his warm, strong hands holding her.

Nick flourished his arm grandly as he stepped aside. She saw behind him now, the white horse tethered to a white carriage. A small, elderly woman dressed in a tuxedo, tipped her black top hat to Dakota as she held open the door.

Dakota, who felt as if her mouth had been hanging open for too long, started laughing in disbelief. "You did *not* just show up in a horse-drawn carriage!"

"Ladies first," he responded as he helped her in.

They sat close to one another, legs tucked under a thick blanket as the carriage rolled slowly through Central Park. The city lights reflected off the buildings and snow-covered landscape.

"I feel as if we're riding through a postcard," Dakota said dreamily, as she gazed out the window. She had her head on Nick's shoulder.

"It's a real winter wonderland, isn't it?" he asked her.

She smiled at his reference to the song that had drawn them together yesterday, "There's certainly no lack of sleigh bells or glistening snow," she agreed. "Thanks so much for the grand tour. I'd say you earned an A+ in "Sweeping Her Off Her Feet 101."

He shifted to face her as she lifted her head.

"Look, Dakota, as long as we are speaking in Christmas carol-ese, let me just take it to the next level of corniness, and tell you I've been conspiring with people in my line of work today."

She looked at him, feeling curious, "All you've told me about your 'line of work is that you're a glorified paper-pusher. So tell me, what was the buzz around the water cooler today?"

He hesitated before answering, "I may have understated my position. The truth is, I've pretty much clawed my way to the top of the paper-pushing food chain. The water cooler sits in my huge corner office which boasts a million-dollar view of America's most vibrant city." he paused as he tried to read her face. "I'm telling you this, not to impress you with my resume, but as a means of illustrating that I know my industry."

"OK, I get it," she told him, "but what exactly *is* your industry?"

"Let me put it this way -- last night when I heard you sing, I knew immediately that your voice is special. That's not a sappy sentimentality from a boy who is falling in love with a pretty girl. It's a professional assessment from a man who enjoys the view from his 28th-floor glass office at Atlantic Records," he finished and waited for her reaction

Dakota couldn't help herself as she blurted, "So, is that what this is all about? You're courting me like royalty because you think I can make you more money? This is how you built your career?" She felt as if the last 24 hours had been an emotional rollercoaster ride.

He responded calmly, "I have no intention of making a dime from your singing. What I am trying to tell you is that I have spoken with a producer friend over at Virgin Records. I gave him the heads up that you were playing tonight and suggested that he might want to listen in. Long story short, he visited the coffee shop this evening. What happens next is entirely between you and him," he said as he reached for her hand.

"I don't think you are the type of girl who can be bought, Dakota. It's like I told you last night--when I'm with you, I feel something that I used to think was silly sentimentality. I wouldn't trade that for any number of additional zeros on my income statement."

Dakota returned his soul-searching gaze for nearly a minute before she grinned and said simply, "I'll bet you say that to all the girls."

The carriage had slowed to a stop and the driver turned in her seat to ask loudly, "What's next on the agenda, Prince Charming?"

Nick looked at Dakota and winked before answering the grandmotherly driver, "Home."

He took Dakota's hands and said, "I'm pretty handy at flipping the switch that stokes a roaring blaze in my apartment's gas fireplace. Care to join me on the hearth for a nice chardonnay?"

Her kiss was all the answer he needed.

A TIFFANY'S CHRISTMAS

CHAPTER 1

*T*here was nothing quite like Christmas at Tiffany's.

Year upon year, Naomi was captivated by the magic of the iconic NYC jewelry store. Even before she stepped inside, the beautifully intricate and captivating holiday windows transported her to another world, filled with festive glamor and wonder.

A real-life fairytale, right there on Fifth Avenue.

And once she stepped through those revolving doors and came out the other side, the everyday hustle and bustle of Manhattan melted away and she was in wonderland.

Holly Golightly was right; nothing bad could truly ever happen at Tiffany's.

And for Naomi, only good things had.

Her mom used to work as a store assistant at the flagship store, and as a little girl, Naomi would come here to visit Amelia while she worked.

At Christmastime there was simply no better place to be than by the glittering display counters, watching her mom help customers choose their perfect purchase.

She couldn't in a million years afford some of the items she sold, but that was never a concern. Her mom just loved making other people happy, and helping to find a gift that was just right for that special someone was enough to make her day, every day.

Sadly Amelia was no longer around to do that, but by returning here every year during the holidays Naomi felt like she was holding on to that childhood memory, and keeping it alive.

Now, she looked at surrounding spruces adorned with Tiffany's signature little blue boxes, each standing as a regal centrepiece for each of the central display cases on the ground floor. Illuminated lighting and additional silver and robin's egg-coloured blue baubles completed the look to perfection.

Wreathes, similarly decorated in inimitable Tiffany's style, lined the walls of polished wood and dark green marble interspersed between the panels.

This year, a huge Tiffany-blue advent calendar stood sentry at the front entrance, and Naomi could only guess at the luxurious treasures to be revealed beneath each door throughout the Christmas countdown.

'You really would've loved this year's décor Mom,' she whispered to herself as she strolled casually along the glass display cabinets, marvelling at the stunning jewellery.

But Naomi was never there to shop. She just came to remember.

And in a way, continue the tradition her parents had started when she was just a toddler. She still remembered clinging excitedly to her dad's hand as every year he spirited her through the doors of the store's glittering wonderland, before heading straight toward her mother's post.

After the visit, the two of them would stroll further up the street as far as Rockefeller

Center, taking in the famed Fifth Avenue holiday displays along the way.

There, father and daughter would spend time gliding on the ice before enjoying steaming hot chocolate and gawping in wonder at the mammoth Christmas tree.

Reliving that same tradition every year (albeit alone) was pretty much all Naomi needed to make this time of year perfect.

And these days she felt she needed it more than ever.

Christmas was supposed to be a time of kindness, joy and compassion, but there was little of that in the air this year.

As an *NYCTV News Today* reporter, she should know. It was Naomi's job to find interesting local news to share with the city, but recently her stories were getting bleaker and bleaker.

She didn't want to spend another second thinking about muggings and officer-involved shootings, and she'd had more than enough of burglaries and attacks. To say nothing of politics.

It was Christmas week and Naomi just wanted something escapist and inspiring.

Tiffany's was exactly that.

There were so many good memories here. It was far more than just a store. Time spent within these walls helped shape her life in more ways than one.

In a way, it had inspired her career. The stories her mother used to impart about her work days, so many tales of romance and joy behind those famous little blue boxes, had lit a fire under Naomi's own fascination with finding the extraordinary within the ordinary, and partly the reason she'd become a specialist in human interest stories.

Today, the store's ground floor was filled with shoppers seeking out Christmas gifts in time for the big day next week.

Naomi glanced at an elegant woman nearby whose neck was adorned with a vintage fur stole. Her silver hair was pinned up in a neat French twist, and large pearl earrings dangled from her wrinkled ears.

She reminded her of a character from one of those old musicals she and her mother loved to watch, and Naomi hummed to herself as she moved on, watching people jauntily swinging the store's signature blue bags.

She spied a little girl with big chocolate curls around her ears and a bright red woollen hat on her head, holding her father's hand, scampering behind him as he strolled along the glass display cases. The child looked a lot like Naomi when she was about that age, though her own hair was considerably longer now and her eyes hazel while the little girl's eyes were blue.

Time goes by so fast.

She still couldn't believe that in a few short months, she'd be saying goodbye to her thirties and hello to her forties.

She loosened her green-check scarf as she stopped to look at a beautiful gold necklace with a twist knot pendant. It was beautiful and exactly the kind of thing she would choose for herself.

If I could afford it...

Still, Naomi was more than content to just look and admire the exquisite piece, until just out of her peripheral vision, something caught her attention.

A man was coming through the revolving doors. He was tall, tanned, and very handsome with dark brown hair and a concerned look on his face - but it wasn't so much his distinguished appearance than his harried, uncertain expression that had caught her eye.

That and the fact that he'd come *in* with a Tiffany's bag, not out, which alerted her to the fact that something was off.

He was so focused, that unlike anyone else who entered the store, he didn't pause to admire the unmissable advent calendar, nor check out any of the displays; he just kept striding past counter after counter.

Her journalist radar well and truly pinging, it wasn't long before Naomi was doing the same.

Intrigued, she followed along as a Tiffany's assistant clad in formal attire, pointed him in the direction of the elevators at the back of the shop floor - and quick as you like, Naomi hurried her pace toward the already retracting doors.

CHAPTER 2

'Wait!' Naomi called out, stepping in behind the man just before the doors closed.

She flushed a little as the elevator attendant smiled a greeting.

'Which floor are you visiting today?' he asked politely and she repeated what she'd heard the man utter just as she stepped inside. 'Fourth, please.'

Arriving at that floor, they both stepped out, the man graciously allowing Naomi to depart first, despite his obvious haste.

He then headed directly toward the Guest Services desk, while she meandered idly between the shelves, pretending to look at one item or another, as she drew closer.

There was a display of leather wallets just a couple of feet away from the desk, just close enough for her to listen in without being obvious.

'May I help you?' a smiling store assistant asked from nearby, and Naomi cursed inwardly behind her smile.

'I'm good, thanks. Just browsing.'

'Of course. Let me know if you need anything.'

She'd missed his opening gambit at the desk but noticed that the man was gesturing toward the bag, while the Guest Services lady looked on with a puzzled frown.

The assistant then opened the bag and withdrew the contents; the store's unmistakable blue box; this one elongated and rectangular.

But instead of the also-typical Tiffany white satin ribbon and bow, this was wrapped in holiday red; a more festive deviation for this time of year, Naomi knew.

'I'm sorry, sir, but I'm afraid I can't help you,' she heard the assistant say. 'If there was a receipt I'd be able to check the system, but without one, there's just no way of telling ...'

'But there has to be *some* way of finding out who lost it,' the man was insisting. 'It could be very valuable and likely intended as a Christmas gift.'

A lost gift....? Now well and truly intrigued, Naomi drifted even closer.

'Please ... is there maybe a list of items sold yesterday that you could check against ... see if something might correspond to a box this size? Someone is surely missing this and I'd really like to get it back to its rightful owner.'

The assistant did well to hide her incredulous expression. 'I'm sorry, sir, but that is impossible. A great majority of our jewellery purchases come in boxes this size, and of course, we have so many such sales coming up to the holiday season ...'

A heavy sigh. 'Which means opening the box wouldn't help us either, though I'd really like to avoid that if I could...' he muttered, his voice trailing off, as he struggled to figure out what to do next.

The assistant smiled politely. 'I'm so sorry we can't help, but I'm sure the owner will come back once they've realized they've left it behind,' she offered and he nodded despondently.

Naomi's heart raced as her mind began figuring out the basics of the situation.

And she recognized an opportunity.

'Excuse me ...' She stepped closer to the desk just as the man was walking away, and he and the Tiffany's assistant both turned to look at her. 'Sorry to interrupt, but I couldn't help but overhear your conversation,' she explained, indicating the box and bag. 'Something's been lost?'

The man's green eyes widened with interest, and some reserve too.

'Might you be the owner?' he asked cautiously.

'Oh no, I'm afraid not,' she told him. 'I just thought I might be able to help.'

'Really? How so?'

She extended her hand. 'My name's Naomi Stewart and I'm a reporter with *NYCTV News*.'

'Oh I thought I'd seen you before,' the Tiffany's assistant called out warmly. 'I love your segments.'

Naomi smiled. 'Thank you.' She fell into

step beside the man as he walked away. 'If you let me know the circumstances, perhaps I might be able to help you find the owner, Mr...'

'Ricci. My name is Raymond Ricci. I just don't see how,' he replied, though she could tell that thanks to the assistant's recognition, he was no longer quite so suspicious of her. 'Someone left their Christmas shopping behind in a café. Not exactly a thrilling news story.'

'Well, that depends on how you look at it,' Naomi said, ambling alongside him as they headed back to the elevators. 'Somebody out there is surely missing it, or perhaps might not yet have even realized they've left it behind - or where. I was thinking that maybe you might consider making a public appeal via our news channel. If *NYCTV* could help find the owner and reunite them with the gift in time for the holidays, it would make for a wonderful feel-good segment.'

'But anyone could claim to be the owner,' Raymond questioned. 'And I don't even know what the box contains. To say nothing of the fact that whatever's inside is none of my business; it's just lost property from my café.'

'You own the café it was left in?'

'Yes, one of my wait staff found it beneath a table yesterday and brought it straight to me. We were hoping that someone would've come back for it by now, but nobody has. I don't want something so potentially valuable lying around my premises, so I thought I'd come to Tiffany's to see if they could shed any light. But there was no receipt in the bag, so we're all still in the dark.'

His brow wrinkled and Naomi couldn't help but notice that he really was very handsome. Those arresting green eyes stood out against his strong jawline and sallow skin.

"I'm pretty sure I can weed out any timewasters. We have a nose for that in my line of work,' she explained with a grin. 'Comes with the territory.'

He nodded. 'OK, so if I were to do this ... how would you want to work it? I'd really love to find the owner as soon as possible.' Raymond looked at her and she also noticed the determination in his piercing gaze. 'It's Christmas week after all.'

'Actually, I think the timing will only enhance people's eagerness to get involved,' she told him, eagerly. 'We can filter the calls through the station and I can question responders before presenting any leads to you. Let me help you with this, so you can focus on your business Mr Ricci. I've been looking for a feel-good Christmas segment. Goodness knows this city needs it.' She smiled brightly. 'What do you say?'

He looked thoughtful for a moment, then an acquiescent smile spread across his face. 'I guess we can give it a shot - what have we got to lose? And please, call me Raymond.'

'Great,' Naomi grinned happily, eager to get cracking. 'I already have a couple of ideas about how to frame the story to weed out time-wasters. But first, I need you to help me set the scene by laying out exactly how you came to find the gift and where. Do you have time to maybe grab a coffee somewhere?'

'Sure,' Raymond replied with a smile. 'I know just the place.'

CHAPTER 3

*H*e led Naomi straight to the 'scene of the crime'; a cosy traditional Italian café called Caffe Amore, located on a quiet little corner between Fifth and Madison.

Simple in décor with polished wood and black and white tiled floors, patrons were enjoying food on checkered cloth-covered tables and wrought-iron chairs sipping coffee, or indulging in some very appealing-looking sweet treats.

Behind the old-style glass-fronted cabinets was a seemingly endless variety of freshly-made pastas, sandwiches and pastries, as well as a gelato fridge.

On the walls, Naomi noticed some very old

photographs of the place down through the years, signifying a family-run establishment that had lasted through the ages.

The café was warm, inviting and full of character, the kind of place anyone would be happy to while away the hours, and she immediately understood how someone could get so comfy and cosy here that they'd easily lose track of time, let alone belongings.

Raymond led her to a small table for two by the window and sat down across from her, setting the Tiffany's bag on the table between them.

Naomi unwrapped her scarf from around her neck, set her coat on the back of her chair, then took out her phone and put it on the table, ready to record their conversation.

He signalled to a waitress. 'Coffee? And maybe something to eat while you're here?' He indicated the display cabinet. 'Go ahead. Pick whatever you want, tiramisu, cannoli …'

'You shouldn't say that,' Naomi joked. 'I can eat a *lot*.'

He raised an eyebrow. 'I like a woman who enjoys her food.'

She met his gaze as her heart fluttered a

little in her chest. He was *very* handsome, and her first instinct about his Italian heritage was correct.

But she was here for a story, not a date. She needed to remember that.

She decided on coffee and traditional cannoli, and got straight down to the specifics, getting all the details she needed to lay the groundwork for the news segment and appeal.

But when the cannoli arrived and she took her first bite of the delicate almond pastry, Naomi almost forgot to focus on his words.

'Oh my, this is ... incredible,' she said, as the creamy mascarpone filling permeated her senses. 'I've had cannoli downtown, but this is something else.'

Raymond chuckled; a deep, rich rumble that she liked. It reminded her a little of her dad's laughter.

'My own recipe,' he told her proudly, before adding with a wink. 'Sicilians do it better.'

Naomi could have sworn he was flirting with her and couldn't deny that she quite enjoyed the prospect. But then she reminded herself that Raymond Ricci was Italian, so of *course* he was. Flirting was practically in his blood; it had nothing to do with her.

Did it?

'So, back to the story …' she said, swallowing hard.

CHAPTER 4

*T*he following day, everything was set.

Naomi pressed her lips together to spread lipstick evenly over them as she checked her reflection.

'You truly are a magician, Jill,' she commented to the make-up artist.

'Honey, if all of my clients had your face to work with, every job would look this good,' Jill mused. The petite redhead had started working for the station a month after Naomi joined five years before.

Since then they'd become best friends, and Jill was the only artist she allowed to do her makeup.

'Stop, you flatter me.'

'No, I enhance you. That's what a good makeup artist does.' Jill began to pack away her kit. 'And I really hope you get to the bottom of this mystery. It's such a great idea for a story. Really Naomi, with your looks and knack for sniffing out leads, you really should be on CNN or something.'

'You know I'm happy here,' she replied.

It was the same discussion they'd been having for years. Jill thought she could do better. Naomi was content with what she had, though one day, she'd like to get behind the camera and produce.

And she didn't want to do hard news either. Human interest stories were her thing.

'Is Mr Ricci here?' she asked turning in the revolving make-up chair. She was dressed in a tasteful jade green suit with a red button-down on the inside and white pearl earrings. Her dark-brown curls were pinned up in a messy bun, with tendrils framing her face, and her TV makeup glow and understated.

'You mean Romeo? I'm heading down now to give him a touch-up on set,' Jill said with a wink. 'You sure you know how to pick the guys too - he is *hot*.'

'Stop it, it's not like that,' Naomi insisted, but there was no mistaking the fact that Jill was right. The main player in her latest news story was indeed hot.

Which could only serve to increase the public response to it.

IN THE STUDIO, Naomi weaved between cameras and stepped over large cables on the way to her position.

Raymond was already in place and looked nervous as she approached. His foot bounced repeatedly and his hands were flat on his knees.

He combed his fingers through his dark hair, first smoothing it back and the next minute ruffling it afresh.

She smiled a little, remembering how nerve-wracking her first time on camera had been, but it was cute to see such a confident man so out of his comfort zone.

The set for this segment was festively deco-rated with plastic gingerbread men in white-trimmed clothing and green and red 'sugar drop' eyes. The border was trussed up with candy-cane-coloured trim to represent roof shingling, along with a 'blazing' fire in the corner and a cheery Christmas tree in the corner to top it all off.

'You'll be fine,' Naomi reassured Raymond as she took her place across from him.

'I have never been this nervous in my life,' he admitted. 'I can't keep still.'

'I know what's like. Believe me. Try to think of this as just a conversation between the two of us, like yesterday in your café. Forget the cameras. You just concentrate on me.' She smiled. 'I'll get you through this in one piece. I promise.'

He took a deep breath. 'I just hope it works,' he said, indicating the Tiffany's bag sitting on a small table in front of them.

They'd decided to show viewers the bag, but not the contents. One element of Naomi's plan to weed out any time-wasters.

'I know you do. So do I. That's why we're here after all.' She placed a hand on his. 'You'll be fine.'

'Of course he will!' Jill interrupted exuberantly. 'He's got you.' The make-up artist turned to Raymond. 'I'm Jill and I'm going to touch you up.'

'Excuse me...?'

Naomi had to laugh at his expression.

'Nothing much, just a little powder to cut down on the shine.' Jill smirked. 'Trust me, honey, a face like yours doesn't need much enhancement.' She turned to wink again at Naomi, who tried not to blush.

Raymond just shrugged. 'Whatever you say.'

CHAPTER 5

$\mathcal{M}$inutes later, the segment was underway.

'Today, I have in-studio, a real-life Santa Claus of sorts,' Naomi smiled to the camera before turning to Raymond. 'Mr Ricci, thank you for being with us on *NYCTV News Today*.'

'It's my pleasure.'

'We're so happy to have you with us. But maybe start by telling us why are you here?'

His nerves suddenly forgotten, Raymond went on to tell the story of how the Tiffany's bag had been left behind in his Manhattan business. Again, upon Naomi's advice, they had agreed to leave out many of the specifics, such as the location and indeed the name of the café

- so as to ensure that they could weed out the time-wasters and correctly identify whomever came forward. Only the true owner would be able to fill in the blanks.

Naomi raised the Tiffany bag to the camera for viewers to see, while Raymond outlined what they had agreed to share.

'I thought the owner might come back for it, but a day later nobody had, so I went to Tiffany's to see if I could maybe track someone down that way. I didn't open the box and I don't want to. After all, it's meant for someone special. It wouldn't be right to open someone else's gift.'

Then Naomi faced the camera. 'When we at *NYCTV News Today* heard about Raymond's predicament, and his heartfelt determination to have the gift returned to its rightful owner, we had to help. That's why today we are appealing for that person - or anyone who might have more information - to contact us here in studio so that we can ensure that you, or your special someone, is reunited with this wonderful gift in time for Christmas. The number to call is on your screen now. *NYCTV News* will remain closely involved in the hunt all the way, and will of course keep you advised of what we hope will be a happy ever after to this story. Thank you for watching. I'm Naomi Stewart.'

'And we're out.'

At the edge of the set, her producer flashed two thumbs up and Naomi turned to Raymond, who looked relieved.

'That wasn't so bad.'

'Told you I'd make it easy on you.'

'You were right,' he said, meeting her gaze. 'You really do have a way of making people feel like there's nobody else in the room.'

As he said this, her heart skipped a beat, but then she reminded herself that he was talking about her talent as an interviewer, nothing more.

The sound team came up to remove their mics as Naomi and Raymond got to their feet.

'How long do you think before people start calling?' he wondered.

'Knowing these things, I'm pretty sure the phone's already hopping,' she told him. 'You were great on camera.'

'Thank you so much for doing this. I appreciate your help. I don't know what I would have done if I hadn't bumped into you - in Tiffany's I mean.'

'You're welcome,' she said with a soft laugh. 'And like the story goes ... nothing bad ever happens there. Let me walk you out. It can get pretty confusing out back.'

She started to lead him away from the set and Raymond followed. 'You know, I never even asked why you were there that day.'

Naomi shrugged. 'Revisiting old memories,' she admitted simply, and when he looked confused she decided to tell him about her parents, and how going there every Christmas was her way of remembering.

'Kind of tradition, I guess. Like that slogan they have on their stuff; 'Return to Tiffany's.' I keep returning there every year to remember.' Then she laughed self-consciously, realizing how stupid it all must sound.

But Raymond looked thoughtful. 'No, I get it,' he said quietly, looking sideways at her. 'Family traditions are so important, especially at this time of year. And for what it's worth, I think your folks would be very proud.'

*T*he response to the slot was immediate and unprecedented. Calls started to flood into the station from people insisting they were the ones who'd lost the gift and wanted to get it back.

It was easy to tell from the get-go which were frauds based on Naomi's three main criteria: either the timing was wrong, they couldn't identify the location as Caffe Amore or the fact that the box in question was not the traditional Tiffany's square-shaped 'little blue box' but long, rectangular and wrapped with a red ribbon instead of white.

But they did get one early response that seemed genuine, and when Naomi went to check it out in person, her producer insisted on sending a cameraman to the woman's home to capture the happy moment live, just in case.

'And the Italian guy too if you can swing it. The camera loves him.'

Naomi couldn't argue with that, and for his part, Raymond had also been insistent about making sure they had the right person before handing the gift over.

Now they climbed the steps of the Brooklyn apartment, the camera guy bringing up the rear.

'Do you really think this could be it?' Raymond asked.

'I hope so.'

'I still can't believe the response,' he continued, shaking his head. 'It's great, but who knew so many people could be so dishonest?'

She sighed. 'I wish I could say I'm surprised, but I'm not. I've been working in news for a long time now and I've learned not to expect too much.'

'Saves you the disappointment, huh?'

Naomi shrugged. 'I've gotten used to the

depressing stuff, but still, you always need to try to find the light.' She smiled. 'That's why this whole thing drew me in. It was a chance to showcase something good when lately all we've been getting is the bleak and dreary. I wanted to give New Yorkers something to feel good about - especially at this time of year, a holiday story to make them smile.'

'You're really passionate about this, aren't you?'

Their eyes met and again, there was something in the way Raymond looked at her that made her breath catch.

'Of course. As are you.' She chuckled and tucked an imaginary strand of hair behind her ear. 'Shall we go in?'

He nodded, and the three continued up the steps.

A WOMAN OPENED the door on the second knock. She was a tall, slender brunette in her mid-thirties with a gap between her front teeth.

Her makeup was flawless and her clothes stylish, but not expensive designer wear.

'Please, come in,' she invited, and Naomi noted that she seemed far more interested in the cameraman, than the prospect of recovering her lost belongings. 'Oh. I didn't know there'd be cameras. Maybe I should change my clothes...'

'Don't worry, there's no rush just yet,' she assured her. 'Lots of time for that if you'd like, but first we need to ask you a few questions.'

The interior was tasteful but sparsely decorated. If she had to guess, Naomi would bet the woman didn't own it, and from the lack of furniture, couldn't afford to.

'Please have a seat. Can I get you something to drink?' she asked as they walked into the living area. 'Juice, tea or coffee?'

'I'm good,' Raymond replied.

'Me too,' Naomi agreed.

The woman's name was Belinda Brooks, and from what she'd already shared with the station she'd been to Caffe Amore on the correct date and time. It was a promising start but they needed specifics before they went any further.

'Belinda, can you tell us more about your visit to the café that day?' Naomi began.

'It was morning, closer to noon. I was in Tiffany's over on Fifth to pick up a present for my mother. She turns seventy on Christmas Eve and I wanted to get her something special.'

'That's wonderful. Happy Birthday to your mom,' Naomi enthused warmly.

'Thanks. I'll tell her that when I give it to her,' Belinda responded. 'I spent a lot of time there picking it out. I wanted to be sure it was the perfect gift.'

'Of course. Would you mind telling us what it was that you bought?'

The woman frowned then. 'I thought you said on the news that you didn't open the box? So how would you know what was in there?' She looked at Raymond through narrowed eyes. 'Did you open my mom's present?'

'No,' he interjected quickly. 'Of course not. Like I said, I didn't want to intrude on anyone's privacy. But I'm sure you understand that we need to be sure it's being returned to the right person.'

'Right,' Belinda replied with a nervous laugh. 'Understandable I guess. So it was ... a leather purse,' she said, after a beat.

Naomi's spirits sank. 'A purse?' she repeated.

She shared a glance with Raymond, who looked somewhat crestfallen.

'Yes.'

But Naomi didn't give anything away. 'That is a wonderful gift for your mom.'

'I know. So when can I have it back?' Belinda questioned, glancing at the camera. 'Do you wanna do that now? I really should get changed first...'

'We just have to check a couple more things,' Raymond replied before Naomi had a chance to intervene. 'You understand I'm sure, that we'll need to verify a few things.'

Belinda's brow wrinkled infinitesimally. 'And how would you go about that, may I ask?'

'Well, we've got everything we need for the moment. Someone from the studio will be in touch soon.' She stood up.

'But when?' the woman insisted forcefully, getting to her feet too. 'Coming from Tiffany's it wasn't cheap, you know. I need to get it back and you have no right to keep it from me. Who do you think you are?'

Raymond placed a gentle hand on her arm

and his voice was velvety soft as he spoke. 'Don't worry, we'll ensure your mother has a great birthday, Belinda. Why don't you take her down to the café? I'll reserve a table and arrange a special birthday surprise.'

'You would? Thank you … she'd love that. She loves Caffe Amore, we both do.'

'It would be my pleasure to have you both as my guest.'

Naomi marvelled at how calmly he'd disarmed a potentially confrontational situation in the loveliest way.

He really was a nice guy.

*T*he three left the apartment, and no one said anything until they were back out on the street and the camera guy had taken off.

'That was a nice thing you did back there,' Naomi began.

'I recognized her,' Raymond said. 'She comes in to the café every now and again. Never buys much, just a coffee and sits alone with it for hours on end. Get the sense that she doesn't have much money, but is desperate for mom's approval, hence the desire for the gift.'

She looked at him. 'I got that too. About the approval thing I mean. But you were very kind, not only for not calling her out about the gift, but helping her do something special for her mother's birthday.'

He shrugged. 'Happy to.' Then he sighed deeply. 'Not looking good though, is it? Only a few more days left till Christmas.'

'Hey, you and I are on a mission remember? We won't be easily deterred.' Naomi held up her hand for a high five, trying to raise his spirits. 'And we're going see this story through to the end.'

He grinned back. 'To the end,' he agreed, holding his hand up to meet her palm, and as he pulled away accidentally entangled her fingers in his.

Blushing hard, she dropped her hand quickly and fished out her phone.

'So what next then?' Raymond asked. 'Any more promising leads for us to chase down?'

Naomi scrolled through the messages from the production team. 'Lots more, but only time will tell as to whether or not they're promising. I'll go through these at home later,' she told him.

'Or we could go through them together back at the café?' Raymond suggested, with an irresistible smile. 'Food's on me.'

. . .

'DID YOU ALWAYS LOVE TO COOK?' Naomi asked later when Caffe Amore had closed for the day, and it was just her and Raymond out back in the kitchen.

It was late by the time they'd gone through the latest batch of responses to the appeal, so he'd insisted on making her dinner. 'How did that happen?'

'My mom.' Raymond wiped his hands on an apron and planted his huge hands on the stainless steel countertop. 'When I was young I was always in the kitchen with her. I was her 'little helper" he explained. 'My siblings were all a lot older than I was. I was, will we say, an unexpected arrival. The closest, my brother, is ten years older than me.'

Naomi almost choked on her red wine. 'Ten?'

He nodded. 'Yes. My folks thought they were through with children when Mom got pregnant again. She actually thought she was starting the menopause but nope - there I was.'

'Wow. That's amazing,' Naomi laughed. 'I

don't know what I would do if that happened to me. I think I'd be too shocked to even react.'

'You want children?' he asked, his incredible green gaze focused on her. Again, she felt her stomach flip.

'Yeah, I do,' she replied honestly. 'I always wanted to be part of a bigger family. Don't get me wrong, I had an amazing childhood. My mom and dad were wonderful, the best parents you could ask for. They were amazing really, my dad in particular used to talk about always trying to find the magic in every moment, the extraordinary in the every day.' She smiled. 'Like I told you before, Mom worked at Tiffany's and she used to say that there was a story behind every little blue box. It's why I wanted to get so involved in your story. And ..."

Naomi bit her lip and Raymond raised a curious eyebrow. She sighed. 'I guess now would be a good time to come clean about how I did get involved. That day... when you asked why I was there in Tiffany's, I didn't quite tell you the truth. The part about being there to remember my parents was true, but it's not exactly the whole story ...'

She went on to admit that she'd seen him come into the store, and had purposely followed him up to the Fourth Floor.

When she'd finished, Raymond guffawed.

'I *knew* there was something off. It was a bit too convenient that a news reporter "just happened" to overhear my predicament.' He shook his head, chuckling still. 'Wow; you really do have a nose for a story, your folks taught you well. Clearly, we have a lot in common in that regard,' he winked, kneading pasta dough - his mom's recipe.

"So, yeah, it was just me, and as an only child, we get all the attention.' Naomi smiled. 'I wanted siblings but they weren't coming, so I decided that when I got older I'd aim to have a big family of my own.'

'And how is that plan coming along?' He returned to the stove and a sizzling sound filled the air.

'Ha...not so well,' She took another long gulp from her glass. 'My last relationship was a complete disaster. Incompatible doesn't even begin to describe us.'

He raised an eyebrow. 'So how come you got together in the first place?'

'Desperation? Delusion? Pick any 'D.'"

He frowned. 'I don't understand. Why would someone like you be desperate?'

She raised an eyebrow. 'You know, you're asking some very serious questions now. Which one of us is the reporter again?'

He smiled. 'Sorry. I'm a curious guy.'

Naomi shrugged. 'I guess I work a lot,' she admitted. 'The job means long hours, conferences and having to travel all around the city at any hour ... you name it, and as a business owner I'm sure you can imagine how that is. It doesn't always leave a lot of time to date. When I met my last boyfriend it was at a speed-dating thing that a friend invited me to for a charity she worked at. He was nice and pretty decent-looking. So I took a chance. Problem was he wasn't a lot of fun.'

'Sorry it didn't work out.'

'It was for the best. I want the right person. I don't just want anyone. I made a mistake, but at least it wasn't one I had to live with for the rest of my life.'

'Rest of your life?'

'If I'd married him, I mean.'

'You were engaged?'

Naomi laughed. 'No! Thankfully we never got that far.'

A LITTLE WHILE LATER, Raymond began to plate the food. She'd seen everything he'd prepared and was eager to try the finished product.

It was a new recipe he was testing out for the café, and she was going to be the first person to try it.

Turned out that Raymond had based the entire menu at Caffe Amore around his own recipes. There was nothing on it that he hadn't concocted himself. Even the cannoli.

'But do you want to get married?' he asked as he set the pasta bowl on the countertop in front of her and sprinkled herbs over huge chunks of bison meat, something she'd never tried before. But Naomi wasn't afraid to try new things.

She picked up some food but the fork slipped from her hand, and she leaned from the barstool to catch it but underestimated just how far it had dropped. The next thing she knew she was starting to topple over and let out a yelp as she began to fall.

Naomi fully expected to collide with the floor but to her surprise, Raymond's strong hands were suddenly there to catch her.

She still stumbled over but it wasn't nearly as bad as it would have been.

He cradled her in his arms for a beat as she looked up at him with a racing heart. Then she righted herself and stood back, swallowing hard.

'I ... do,' she muttered.

His brow furrowed. 'What?'

'I do ... want to get married - someday,' she blabbered, her heart thundering, as she tried to cover up her embarrassment.

Raymond smiled and took a seat alongside her. 'Me too.'

CHAPTER 8

*W*ork for Naomi had tripled since the segment.

There was so much interest in, not just the gift, but the story too. The slot had since been syndicated to a couple of networks outside of the city, and when that happened, even more responses flooded in.

Her producer, Patrick was over the moon.

'I think you've found your niche,' he commented happily, as she sat in his office, reading over the terms of the new contract she'd just been offered.

'Are you serious?' Naomi stared up at him. 'You're going to allow me to produce a couple of segments too?'

The money element didn't matter so much, and though it wasn't a minor increase, it wasn't what was most important.

She just wanted the opportunity to tell more stories. Thanks to Raymond's lost gift, Patrick was finally giving her that chance and it felt like a dream come true.

He smiled and the light reflected off the bald spot on the top of his head.

'If all goes well when your next contract comes up for negotiation we might add even more. I know you've always wanted to produce. You certainly have the talent, and if it was up to me I'd have made you a producer already. But now the guys upstairs have seen what you can do too. Merry Christmas, Naomi.'

She got to her feet and promptly threw her arms around him. 'Thank you!'

'You're very welcome,' Patrick laughed. 'Now go get me another great story for your next segment.'

'Yes, sir.'

Naomi was still walking on air as she strode from her boss's office back to her desk.

She picked up her phone to check her

messages and her smile grew even larger when she saw that there was one from Raymond.

Meet me at the place where you'll find the Food of Love.

Naomi frowned. Caffe Amore. She'd made that very joke about the place the other night at dinner.

Why did he want her to meet him there? Then a thought struck her; had the person who'd left the bag behind finally returned?

She hurried out to the street to catch a cab, then to her surprise noticed a horse-drawn carriage outside her building, with a curious sign on the side door.

It said: *'Naomi, your carriage awaits.' Raymond.*

Wondering why he figured anyone would ever want to take a carriage ride through the middle of Manhattan, she clambered aboard all the same. The driver seemed to know where to go too.

What on earth are you up to Raymond?

WHEN THEY REACHED the café she saw him waiting outside.

'What's all this?' Naomi asked.

'Since things have been so busy lately, I thought you might be in as much of a need of a break as I am.' He looked at his watch. 'And given it's lunchtime I figured you might have an hour or so to spare.'

His gaze was intense but gentle. It made her stomach feel as if hummingbirds were fluttering around inside it.

What are you doing? This is supposed to be a news story, not a romantic one.

CHAPTER 9

'OK. But why all this?' she indicated the horse and carriage.

'You're the reporter - figure it out,' he said coyly. 'What's colourful yet evergreen? Come with me to the place where it's closest to the sky.'

'OK, I think I get it. Are you making me do some kind of … scavenger hunt?' Delighted by the prospect, she thought for a moment. 'Colorful and evergreen…. the tree at Rockefeller?'

Raymond got in beside her and all too soon they arrived at their destination, just in time to see a large group carolling beneath the towering Christmas tree.

'OK, is there another clue?'

'Of course. Now we go to a place where you're likely to fall, yet most likely to fly.'

She thought again for a moment. 'Hmm ... this one's a little trickier, but I think I got it.' She smiled and looked down upon the ice rink. 'I'm thinking we'll need some skates?'

'Wow, you're good! Come on then.'

Raymond led her out onto the ice with both hands, just like her dad used to. She didn't need any help, she was a decent skater, but there was something about him leading her that felt right. It was a confusing feeling, but she loved it.

They glided out to the middle of the rink. He was a good skater and it wasn't long before he was spinning and twirling around her.

'Okay, showoff,' Naomi teased as she tried to keep pace.

He skated up and they stood face-to-face. 'You should practice more. I can show you a thing or two.'

Her cheeks grew hot. 'Maybe I'll take you up on that.'

'Naomi,' he said as hands gently reached for her waist. 'I know this might be strange, and we haven't known each other long, but I enjoy spending time with you.'

Her heart almost stopped. He smiled and she smiled back and for a moment she felt like a teenager again.

But then her phone rang and recognizing the ring tone as Patrick's, she pulled it out of her pocket, really wishing she didn't have to break the spell.

Still, she couldn't ignore her producer. 'Hey, Patrick. What's up?'

Naomi's eyes widened as she heard the words coming through, and automatically she turned to look at Raymond. 'You're sure?'

Hanging up, she grabbed his hands in delight. 'Guess what? I think we've finally found our person.'

CHAPTER 10

*T*he guy in question, Dominic Anderson, was back at the station, waiting.

He'd seen the syndicated news segment the day before on a sister channel in Connecticut, and had travelled down from Rhode Island to claim the gift.

'Do you really think he's the one?' Raymond queried as he and Naomi hurried into to the studio.

'He got everything right; the name of the café, the box, the ribbon ... and he seems very determined. Patrick said he refused to go anywhere until he saw me personally.' She smiled encouragingly. 'I really hope so.'

'Me too,' Raymond reached for her hand and quickened his pace. It matched the beating of her heart as she rushed along beside him.

They reached Patrick's office where inside, Dominic was waiting for them. He stood up immediately.

'Naomi Stewart.'

'Hello,' she said with a smile, extending her hand and he shook it. 'And this is Raymond.'

'Nice to meet you,' Dominic replied. 'I recognize you from the TV slot. And from Caffe Amore, of course.'

Raymond's eyes widened in mutual recognition. 'And now I recall your face from that day. You ordered a second cannoli.'

Dominic's smile grew wide. 'I was hoping you'd remember me.'

Naomi took a deep breath. This was their guy, she knew it. But still, she needed to get the formalities out of the way.

'Okay, Dominic, let's get down to specifics. What time of day were you at the café?'

'The morning of the 18th. I had some Christmas shopping to do, and I stopped at the café for a break from the crowds. I was there when I got a call from my mom. My brother was involved in an accident back home in Rhode Island and taken to hospital. I just left without thinking to grab a cab to take me back to Grand Central. My brother was the only thing on my mind. I left my shopping on the floor next to my table. I was right at the window by the door, looking out onto the street.'

Naomi's eyes drifted to Raymond. He had even given them the correct table.

'Please, tell me what I need to do to get it back. I had no idea where I'd left it, I thought maybe in the back of a cab, or on the train … and I've been going out of my mind calling all the cab companies. It's an engagement ring for my girlfriend, you see. I'm planning a Christmas proposal.'

Now her heart sank. He'd got everything right so far - except the box.

An engagement ring would not have been wrapped in a rectangular box and red ribbon. The distinctive packaging was all part of Tiffany & Co's legendary little blue box experience.

She turned to look at Raymond, who hadn't appeared to notice the discrepancy. He looked just as excited as Dominic, and now she didn't know how to broach the subject.

She looked at Patrick, who raised his eyebrows in confusion.

When Naomi remained silent, Dominic sat up.

'Oh, and I have the receipt,' he offered suddenly. He reached into this pocket and pulled out a small piece of paper, handing it to Raymond. 'Man, I was so sure I'd never get it back, and after all the trouble I went to - to make it a surprise, I mean. Then my mom told me there was a TV story about a Tiffany's gift lost in New York, so I watched it and realized you were talking about me. I came back down as soon as I could. I've spent the past few days in the hospital with my brother.'

'How is he?' Raymond asked, ever courteously.

'He'll make it. He'll have a long journey but the doctors expect him to make a full recovery.'

'I'm happy to hear that,' Naomi stated. Then she took a deep breath. 'But Dominic, there's just one problem … the box…' She noticed Raymond's gaze on her and hated to be the one to pull the plug on the excitement.

'Oh, that's right!' Dominic laughed uneasily then. 'You guys didn't open the box, did you? So maybe you don't believe me that it was an engagement ring.' He was chuckling now. 'Like I said, I really wanted this to be a surprise, so I asked the guy at Tiffany's to wrap the little blue box in a *bigger* blue box, if that makes sense. So when I give it to Anna - my girlfriend - on Christmas morning, she won't suspect a thing.'

Naomi exhaled a laugh. 'Oh my gosh. Amazing!' She turned to Raymond who was laughing too. 'Dominic, I think you truly are our guy.'

He looked like he might burst with relief.

'Thank you. Thank you so much. I was afraid I'd have to jump through all kinds of hoops and wouldn't be able to get it back in time for Christmas. We've all been through such a tough time lately, and so I wanted to do something memorable.'

The wheels were turning in Naomi's brain as she thought of something.

'Dominic, I know you went to a lot of trouble already, but how would you feel about making your proposal even *more* memorable for your girlfriend?'

'How so?'

'Well, have you ever thought of doing so on national television?' She turned to look at her producer, who was smiling like a Cheshire cat.

Dominic's eyes grew large and his jaw slackened. 'Are you serious?'

'Totally,' Patrick enthused. 'We'd be so honoured to be part of your proposal and make it something you and your fiancée will never forget.'

Naomi smiled at Raymond.

'And I know our viewers would love to see how this story ends.'

CHAPTER 11

A buzz of excitement raced through the studio on Christmas Eve.

It reminded Naomi why she'd started working TV news in the first place; to be a part of magical, feel-good stories like these.

And this had the potential to be one of the nicest she'd ever uncovered.

'Everyone ready?' she asked, passing through the set on her way to make-up.

'All good to go,' Patrick replied. 'This really was a genius find, Naomi.'

'It couldn't have come together better if we planned it,' she commented smiling.

She and Raymond had hardly had a chance

to speak since Dominic had come to claim the gift, but Naomi was pretty sure he'd be here today to see everything through to the end.

The fact that she hadn't heard from him since stung a little, but she tried her best to ignore the feeling and concentrate on the task at hand.

'So are the happy couple here yet?'

'Dominic just got out of make-up,' the production assistant informed her.

'OK, everyone, take your places!' Patrick bellowed. 'It's showtime.'

NAOMI WALKED onto the set and waited for the sound team to wire them all up. She smiled at Dominic as he joined her on the chair opposite.

'Ready?' she winked and he nodded, swallowing hard.

'Good morning New York,' Naomi declared once the cameras began to roll. 'Today, in this very special *NYCTV News* report, we return to the story of the New York café owner, Raymond Ricci, whose act of generosity launched our search for the owner of a

Tiffany's gift left behind in his - aptly named it seems ... ' she added with a chirpy smile, 'Caffe Amore. And we're so happy to report that there's been a major development; we at *NYCTV News Today* have indeed managed to track down the owner! And you'll soon see, as we conclude this happy journey, that there's even more to this Christmas tale. But first let's meet our elusive shopper, Mr Dominic Andersen. Dominic, welcome to the studio.'

'Thank you. It's ...uh...great to be here.' He gulped nervously.

'We're all so happy to finally find you. The response to our appeal was incredible, so it was quite the search,' Naomi informed her audience. 'Some promising leads and interesting stories, but only one true possibility. And Dominic here was so determined to get back his Tiffany's prize - which he'd intended as a Christmas gift for a very special someone - that he didn't just call the station. He came down here from Rhode Island to see us in person. Dominic, tell us the story in your own words.'

'I was desperate,' Dominic said, going into detail about how he'd come to lose the gift, and then about finding it again. And the unique elements that only he would know; the packaging, the timing and of course, Raymond's café.

Then he turned to look toward his girlfriend, who was standing at the edge of the set, looking on. 'There was something special I needed to do this Christmas, and that gift was a major part.'

Naomi smiled. 'That's right. There's still another twist to come in this Christmas tale. 'Anna, can you come and join us on set?'

As intended, Dominic stood up and escorted his now-visibly startled girlfriend onto the set. Then Naomi got to her feet to greet a shell-shocked Anna, while he reached for the rectangular Tiffany box on the table between their chairs.

'Folks, Anna had no idea she'd be on camera today, so forgive her if she's a little bit speechless right now,' she explained. 'Welcome Anna.'

Naomi looked on smiling, as Dominic opened the rectangular box to reveal the smaller, traditional little blue ring box from within, and his girlfriend sucked in a suitably theatrical breath.

'Anna,' he began, getting down on one knee, while everyone else on set looked on. 'I love you. I've loved you every day since we met. I know it's taken a while, and that you thought maybe this would never come, but today is the day. Please, make me the proudest and happiest man in the world by agreeing to be my wife?'

Anna had no words. Tears rolled down her cheeks as she reached for her boyfriend and embraced him, her head nodded fervently.

A moment later Dominic was slipping a magnificent Tiffany diamond ring on her finger, while the entire set erupted in feel-good applause.

Naomi turned to the cameras, genuine tears of emotion in her eyes.

She was delighted for the couple, but deep down she so wished Raymond could've been here too.

He was such a huge part of this story she couldn't believe he hadn't come along to see it through to the end.

'Well, you just saw it here folks, a Tiffany's Christmas and true fairytale ending, happening right here, right now in Manhattan. I'm so happy we at *NYCTV Today News* were able to bring this heartwarming story to you as it happened, and we're especially honoured to have played a part in its happy ending.

We wish Dominic and Anna every happiness. And we wish you - New York - a very Merry Christmas.'

CHAPTER 12

*I*t was wonderful to watch Dominic and Anna walk off set together; her magnificent Tiffany diamond ring on her finger, and the biggest smile on her face.

That moment Naomi decided there would be no more sad stories in her segment.

No more tales of woe and misery.

From now on, she was going to bring nothing but joy and cheer to New Yorkers. She was going to show them that there was still so much good in their incredible, wonderfully diverse city. And it was there to be found in every corner.

She'd already discussed it with Patrick and

he'd agreed. Things were going to change for the better.

LATER THAT EVENING, Naomi was curled up on the couch of her apartment sniffling at *It's a Wonderful Life* on TV, when she got a text from Raymond, similar to the one he'd sent the day he'd arranged the horse and carriage to take her to Caffe Amore and onwards to Rockefeller.

Except this one said. *Meet me at Tiffany's.*

Another scavenger hunt? On Christmas Eve?

Naomi couldn't deny that the prospect of such a thing excited her. Or anything involving Raymond for that matter.

When? she replied.

As soon as you can.

CHAPTER 13

*S*he grabbed a cab and got there within half an hour to find the man who'd barely been out of her thoughts for the last week, standing on Fifth Avenue with a broad smile on his face.

Most of the department stores - including Tiffany's - had now closed for the holidays, so the streets were calm and quiet. And was it her imagination or was there a hint of snow in the air?

'Hey, Naomi.'

'What's going on?' she asked, shivering a little in the cold. Or was it nervousness? 'How come you weren't there for the broadcast earlier? And what are we doing *here?*' she questioned.

She tucked her hair behind her ears, now wishing she'd bothered to brush it before she came out. Or that she'd hadn't removed her TV make-up.

She must look an absolute mess.

'It's Christmas Eve remember - I couldn't possibly get away from the café today; we were run off our feet. But don't worry, I watched it all on TV. It was wonderful. Well done.'

'Well done you, you mean. It was your story after all.'

'Nope. You were the one who took my petty little problem and turned it into something uplifting.' He reached into his pocket and took something out. 'And for that, I wanted to say thank you.'

Her eyes widened as she caught sight of yet another Tiffany's blue box.

'Raymond ... what's this?'

'A gift of course.'

'Well, I can see that,' Naomi sputtered in disbelief. 'But you really shouldn't have.'

Her eyes were still trained on the blue box. What could be inside, she had no idea.

'Open it.' He held it out to her.

'Raymond ...' she said hesitantly. 'I don't know that I deserve this. I think it might be too much.'

'You do deserve it and it's not too much,' he countered. 'Because of you, two people got a very happy ending this Christmas. It couldn't have happened without you.' He chuckled. 'You restored my faith in people, you know. There was no way I would have ever found Dominic if you hadn't offered to help me.' His voice softened and he reached for her hand. 'And I'm very glad you did, for more reasons than one.'

Her mind was in conflict and her hands were shaking as she took the box from him. She couldn't believe it. Raymond had actually bought her a gift - and from Tiffany's of all places.

It felt like treasure in her hands.

Naomi stared at the box for several long seconds while she contemplated untying the ribbon.

Finally, she decided to just go for it, and unfastening the bow and opening the box, she pulled out the tiny blue jewellery pouch that lay inside.

Tipping it out to reveal what was inside, her

eyes widened when she spied a delicate silver chain and a heart-shaped pendant marked with the famous 'Return to Tiffany's' inscription.

'I remember what you said,' Raymond explained, his voice soft. 'About returning here every year to honour your family tradition.'

Overwhelmed, she looked at him in disbelief, and tears sprang to her eyes. 'This is … amazing. But you shouldn't have.'

'I wanted to,' he said, reaching for her hand again. 'Naomi, I don't think you realize what this time with you has meant to me. You look for the good when people expect bad.'

She swallowed as he placed her hand over his heart. Hers was stampeding with each word he uttered.

'I'm not entirely sure how our lives got entangled for this little adventure, but I'm inclined to think it was for a reason. And it all started right here.' He nodded up at the Tiffany's store.

She smiled, thinking of her parents, their stories and memories and her yearly tradition.

It was as if Raymond had wrapped all of those things up in that single blue box.

'I know.'

He stepped closer.

'I care about you, and I love that you value tradition and memory. And I got you that pendant because I was kind of hoping that you might consider making some new Christmas traditions - with me.'

Now Naomi's cheeks were burning hot. She could hardly look at him as she tried to suppress a grin. She failed miserably and instead decided to just say what she felt.

'I'd ... like that a lot.'

His broad grin matched hers. 'Then there really is just one more thing to do. Merry Christmas, Naomi.'

She gasped as Raymond stepped forward and eliminated the space between them, and Naomi only barely got the words out before their lips met, and her eyes closed.

'Merry Christmas.'

FROM THE AUTHOR

Thank you for reading this festive NYC Christmas collection, I hope you enjoyed it.

If you'd like to read more from me, try a short excerpt of my latest novel, THE BEAUTIFUL LITTLE THINGS, out now.

THE BEAUTIFUL LITTLE THINGS

The magic was missing . . .

Romy Moore sat at the window chair in her late mother's study and looked out over the nearby woods and forestry trails, appreciating why her mum had always found this spot so peaceful.

The trees wore a light dusting of white, the family home's elevated position in the Dublin Mountains ensuring they always got a bit of proper snow in winter, as opposed to the typically damper stuff on lower ground.

Fittingly beautiful for the season, but also serving merely to highlight the fact that everything felt so . . . wrong.

Romy's world was so out of kilter now that

it should be howling gales and driving rain out, not Christmas-card perfection. It made everything even more desperately hollow and painful, and now she understood why some people found this time of year so difficult. The forced festive gaiety, the crippling sense of nostalgia and the idea that everything was supposed to be so bloody *wonderful*. When all she wanted to do right then was pull the covers over her head like it was just another day, a normal day, and she didn't have to pretend to be OK, to try to cheer up and put a brave face on for anyone else's sake.

And most of all, not to have to lie to herself that this time of year, to say nothing of *life*, could ever be the same without her mother.

Romy turned back to the desk and opened up a drawer, seeking a tissue. She found an already open packet of Kleenex and paused a little, reflecting that her mum would've likely used the one just before it, oblivious to the fact that her youngest would be needing the next to grieve her passing.

She wiped her eyes and then blew her nose into the tissue, looking idly through bits and pieces scattered across the desk before coming across a prettily patterned notebook beneath some letters.

Opening the cover, she saw her mother's familiar neat handwriting swirl into focus, achingly comforting, and as she began to read the opening words on the page, Romy quickly realised it was one of her journals.

Her mother loved to write and had kept a journal for as long as Romy could remember – ever the traditionalist at heart, despite her sister Joanna's grand attempt a couple of years back to move her into the twenty-first century with the gift of an iPad.

Feeling like an interloper for even daring to read – these were her mother's private thoughts, after all – she couldn't help but be drawn in, desperate to feel close to her once more.

If you are reading this, then for certain I am no longer with you.

In body at least.

Indeed, it is hard for me to be writing this now, from a place where I am still full of the joys, having just watched you all depart our very last family Christmas together.

While this year's gathering was, in a word . . .

eventful, it gives me such joy that all ended happily – just as I'd hoped.

I wish I could imagine how your lives have been since – and, admittedly, I have tried – but when I attempt to imagine any scenarios that have transpired in the interim, I tend to go down a rabbit hole and overwhelm myself.

I cannot control what will happen. Just as I cannot see the future, I have no way of knowing how any of you will handle my passing.

The only thing I can do from this vantage point right this minute is provide my thoughts, my words, and perhaps a little bit of motherly advice.

I'm trying to picture you all together this time next year without me – and truth be told, I struggle with the concept because it feels so foreign.

So bear with me, as I seek to find the words and comb the recesses of my mind for any wisdom or reminders that might be useful as you navigate the festive period without me.

Firstly, it's OK to feel sad . . . but not forever.

And please do not let grief colour the first Christmas where I am absent. Whatever you do, don't allow sorrow to serve as the backdrop.

Because, oh my darlings, it is still the absolute

best time of year and as you know has always been my favourite.

So please, for my sake, celebrate this Christmas as if I was still here?

Because I will be, in my own way – in all the little festive traditions we have followed over the years, and recipes and rituals that have become our family's staples.

Yes, of course this will be a Christmas like no other.

But that doesn't mean it has to be a terrible one.

It was like . . . a gift, Romy thought, a lump in her throat; though obviously not for her alone.

Because of course her mother would have understood that the family's first holiday period without her would be impossibly difficult.

Though she couldn't possibly have known just how scattered and broken they'd all become since her passing.

But maybe . . . Romy thought, sitting up straight as an idea struck her, and her mind raced as she flicked through the pages, desperate to read more of her mother's wisdom, or any pointers that might help endure her absence.

Maybe this was *exactly* what was needed to mend things – something to gather up all the little broken pieces that were this family now, and help put them back together?

As Romy continued reading, something akin to hope blossomed within her for the first time all year, as she realised that this was the miracle she'd been searching for.

Thank you, Mum. I think I know what to do . . .

While this family might be sinking beneath the surface at the moment, perhaps, with a little guidance, there was hope for them yet.

END OF EXCERPT.

Continue reading THE BEAUTIFUL LITTLE THINGS - out now in ebook, paperback and audio.

ABOUT THE AUTHOR

International #1 and USA Today bestselling author Melissa Hill lives in County Wicklow, Ireland.

Her page-turning contemporary stories are published worldwide, translated into 25 different languages and are regular chart-toppers in Ireland and internationally.

A movie adaptation of SOMETHING FROM TIFFANY'S - a Reese Witherspoon x Hello Sunshine production - is due for world-wide release in Dec, 2022.

THE CHARM BRACELET and A GIFT TO REMEMBER (plus sequel) were also adapted for screen, and multiple other projects are currently in development for film and TV.

www.melissahill.info

Printed in Great Britain
by Amazon

34601233R00149